WYOMING DRIFTER

Dave Gunnison didn't drift up to Wyoming looking for trouble—but he found trouble gunning for him.

Bloodhound deputy sheriff Newton Thomas was on his trail for a Cheyenne bank robbery that Dave got fast-talked into. Thomas needed Dave as his ticket to a full sheriff's star—dead or alive, it didn't matter.

Only homesteader Nathan King offered Dave shelter—if he helped King fend off an army of hired guns in the Johnson County range war. It was the dirtiest fight the West had ever known, and Dave was smack on the firing line.

Dave Gunnison had drifted into a Wyoming death trap— and he had to shoot his way out . . .

WYOMING DRIFTER

Ray Hogan

GUNSMOKE

This hardback edition 2007
by BBC Audiobooks Ltd
by arrangement with
Golden West Literary Agency

ISBN 978 1 405 68138 4

British Library Cataloguing in Publication Data available.

Printed and bound in Great Britain by
Antony Rowe Ltd., Chippenham, Wiltshire

for . . .
EUGENE J. BUIE

1

"Over here! Over here!"

Dave Gunnison came awake instantly at the urgent shout. Rolled up in his blanket and tarp, he hastily threw the covers aside and sat up. It was just daybreak and a cold, early April hush lay over the Wyoming flats and hills, and other than the strident words, the only other sound audible to him was the quiet purling of the Powder River near which he had made his night camp.

"Here—dammit! Circle in."

The angry, impatient demand brought Gunnison to his feet, anxiety sharpening his senses. The voice had come from the opposite end of the brush stand some forty or fifty feet east of where he had made his bed. It could be only cowhands popping strays out of the dense growth—or it could be the Cheyenne posse closing in on Luke Redfern or Hardrock Madden, or possibly both. He hoped that was not it.

The three of them had scattered immediately after the attempt to rob the Cheyenne bank— during which the fourth member of their party,

Charlie Watson, had gotten himself killed—and were off well ahead of the sheriff's posse they knew would quickly organize and follow.

They'd planned well what they would do after the robbery. Madden, who grew up in Wyoming and knew the country, directed them to follow along the east side of the mountains—the Medicine Bows—and make their way separately north to the end of the range. Reaching there, they were to continue on in the same direction until they came to a scatter of low formations folks called Pumkin Buttes.

But they'd best not make the buttes their rendezvous; they'd still be a hundred miles short of the Montana Territory border and the safety Hardrock promised they would find across the line in the badlands. Instead, they were to push on, follow the Powder River until they reached its junction with a stream known as Crazy Woman Creek, which would come in from the west—their left. They could hole up there, figuring themselves fairly safe once they had reached that point.

Dave hadn't reached Crazy Woman Creek yet, although, figuring the number of days he'd been in the saddle since Cheyenne, he reckoned he must be close. And he had thought he was ahead of Hardrock and Luke, but he was now wondering about that.

Pulling on his boots and keeping well back in the brush, Dave put his bedroll together and crossing to where he had picketed his bay gelding and lashed it to the saddle. Returning to where he had made camp, Dave then collected the lard tin in which he'd made coffee, his cup, and what

was left of the rabbit he'd killed and roasted over
the fire that previous night, and thrust it all into
one of the saddlebag pockets.

The attempt to rob the bank had been a complete failure. Not only had Charlie Watson been
killed, but they hadn't gotten a dime out of it.
Two men showing up unexpectedly from a back
room in the building had opened fire on them
before they'd had a chance to grab any money.
The only one to have benefited from the holdup,
Dave had thought bitterly as he made a run for
his horse that morning, was the bank clerk who
had slipped a packet of currency into his pocket
at the height of the excitement planning, no doubt,
to blame its loss on the robbery.

He hadn't been too keen on the bank holdup
idea from the very start, but Madden had figured it all out and it looked like it would be
simple—easy as shooting fish in a barrel, Hardrock
had termed it. The four of them had been together all that winter knocking about in Texas
for a while, then in New Mexico and Colorado
and finally Wyoming, enjoying themselves in the
saloons and having a time with the women. They'd
lived from day to day, taking a job when it became necessary, and one was available, but living
mostly on their luck at the gaming tables. It all
caught up with them in Laramie, where, one
cold morning, they found themselves dead-broke
and almost out of trail grub.

That was when Hardrock came up with a plan
to rob the Cheyenne bank. They'd have plenty of
cash once that was done, and there'd be no sweat
getting away with it; he knew a way to get to the
Montana border unseen, cross over and lie low

for a few days, then go on to a town he called Miles City. They'd have plenty to do in Miles, and if by some bit of hard luck the law caught up with them, they could light out for the Canadian border, cross over, and lose themselves in one of the bigger towns there. Canadian whiskey and women were just as good as those on the American side, Madden had assured them.

Dave wished now he'd objected more strongly to Hardrock's scheme. He should have known it wouldn't be all that easy, but Luke Redfern and Charlie Watson had both thought it was a good plan, and the thing to do—and Madden knew the ropes. He'd been in on a bank robbery before, somewhere in Texas, and everything had gone off without a hitch. There'd been only him and one other fellow, and now, with four men pulling the job, it would be a cinch.

Listening for a few moments and hearing no more from the upper end of the brush stand, Dave took up the reins of his horse, now showing the effects of the long, fast ride from Cheyenne, and swung into the saddle. He'd be ready to move out fast if it became prudent and necessary, but for the time being he'd sit tight, wait, and see what the shouting was all about; as he had thought earlier, it could be just some cowhands rounding up stray cattle.

But Dave Gunnison was finding it hard to accept that possibility. Deep inside him a feeling had sprung to life and steadily strengthened, telling him that Hardrock Madden's plans had gone further awry. Dave swore softly to himself. It seemed to him that nothing had worked out right from the moment they'd set foot inside that bank—and that brought to mind how it had been with the four of them only minutes before they'd made the attempt, waiting there at the edge of town laughing, talking, joshing one another as they made plans for a rosy future.

Madden, sitting tall in the saddle, wide-shouldered, rugged-looking, still wearing the remnants of his army uniform, telling them all how it would be once they got to Miles City; Watson, the kid, the youngest of the bunch, taking it all in, a wide smile on his round, beardless face; Luke Redfern, peaked hat off, red hair shining in the bright Wyoming sunlight, smiling as he told what he would do once he got his hands on a cash stake. He'd stash most of it away in the bottom of his saddlebags for a rainy day, he'd said, and not blow it all at a faro table or on some pretty brunette women.

As for himself, Dave had been no less enthusiastic about prospects than the others. He had laughed and joked with them, related his plans, and even agreed with Redfern that it would be smart to put back some of his share of the money so as not to again find himself flat broke and hungry as he was then.

The only thing that had gone right was their escape from Cheyenne. Forced to leave Watson dead on the floor of the bank, they had managed to get away after throwing a dozen or so shots at the men who had thwarted their plans; they had reached their horses, mounted, separated, and got out of town before the sheriff or anyone else could stop them. Madden had gone west, Redfern east, and he had struck north, just as agreed. Watson, the youngest at sixteen, was to have gone with Madden, the oldest and most experienced at forty, and the most knowing insofar as the country was concerned.

They had been a happy, noncaring bunch, taking life as it came, never worrying as they drifted about the country and looking upon everything in a lighthearted manner. That was all over now, Dave had realized as he was riding north along the Medicine Bows. Charlie Watson was dead; he, Hardrock, and Luke Redfern were now wanted outlaws. Life would never again be the same. They could expect only—

"Thomas! Newt Thomas!" the same voice, now much nearer, suddenly cut into Dave Gunnison's thoughts. "Take your men around the end of them trees and cut in. We've got them in a pocket."

Almost immediately a half-dozen riders, led by one wearing a fringed deerskin coat and a hat with a snakeskin band, rode out of a small stand of trees at the edge of the brush. In that same moment two more riders broke out of the dense growth and, bent low over their saddles, headed for the river.

Dave's jaw tightened as he wheeled his horse about and jerked his rifle from the boot. Madden and Redfern! They were angling across a clearing and coming in his direction. If he could get in a couple of shots at the posse, now streaming out of the trees and the brush farther up and curving in to meet the man called Newt Thomas and his party of lawmen, he might just create enough confusion to enable his two friends to reach the protection of the brush along the river. Throwing up his rifle, Dave aimed at the first of the posse members.

In that same fragment of time a ripple of rifle shots broke out. Hardrock and Redfern abruptly stiffened and drew themselves erect in their saddles as bullets drove into them. Again the rifles crackled. Both men buckled as their horses, almost to the river, slowed. And then, as one, the two men slumped sideways and fell to the ground.

Shocked and filled with a sort of disbelief, Dave slid his rifle back into its boot, dismounted, and, leaving the bay well back in the brush, worked his way forward to where he could see and hear better. He didn't know what he could do for Hardrock or Luke now but he felt he had to stick around and see.

2

Deputy Sheriff Newton Thomas swore deeply as he saw the two riders fall from their saddles and bounce limply when they struck the grassy ground. He had hoped there would be a chance to question them, but Sangaree Dawson, the sheriff and his superior, evidently was in no mind to risk the outlaws escaping a second time and thus had ordered them shot down.

"That makes three of them," Thomas heard Dawson say as with the posse he halted near the lifeless bodies of the two men. "Fourth one's bound to be around here somewheres. Newt, search them good. One of them will have the five hundred dollars they took from the bank."

Thomas climbed down from the buckskin he was riding and crossed to where the outlaws lay. In his mid-twenties, he was a tall, lean man with gray eyes overhung by thick, dark brows. He had a wide mouth, sandy hair and mustache, and unlike the rest of the posse members who, because of the hours on the trail, had forgone the use of their razors, he was clean-shaven—a chore he fulfilled each day regardless of conditions.

14

Dressed in flat-heeled black boots, dark cord pants, blue wool shirt, red neckerchief, gray pinched-crown hat with a snakeskin band, and wearing a lined deerskin coat with an unusually short fringe, he made an impressive figure as he strode toward the outlaws. The butt of the Smith & Wesson .44-40 double-action pistol he carried low on his right hip was visible below the dangling strips of hide, and a bulge in the back of the coat betrayed the presence of a second weapon carried there under his belt.

Bending over the figure of the nearest outlaw, an older-looking man wearing an old army uniform, Thomas examined the corpse thoroughly while Dawson and the posse, near exhaustion from the long ride from Cheyenne, looked on indifferently. The sheriff had pushed them hard in his determination to overtake the bank robbers, and men and horses alike were showing the effects.

Thomas drew himself erect and glanced at Dawson. "Money's not on him," he said, and moved to the other outlaw.

"Any of you recognize these jaspers?" Dawson asked as the deputy began his search of the second body.

There was a murmur of nos. "Sure strangers to me," someone commented.

"I don't figure they're from around Cheyenne or any place close," another rider, wearing his deputy star on the lapel of his red shirt collar, said with a shrug. "One of us would've seen them."

"Yeh, probably rode in from Colorado, or maybe Kansas," a heavy-set man in a dusty business suit remarked. "Plenty of owl hoots running loose in them places."

"Money's not on this one either," Newt Thomas said, coming to his feet.

Sangaree Dawson glanced up into the clear sky at a chevron of geese winging their way northward. Also a tall, spare man, he had small, dark eyes and an intense manner that gave one the impression he was continually beset by serious and weighty problems.

"Dammit," he said feelingly. "Means the fourth one of them's got the money."

"And Lord only knows where he is by now," one of the posse men said wearily.

"Probably headed for Canada," another commented. "Expect that's where they were figuring to join up."

"Hell, let the son of a bitch have it," the heavy-set man in the business suit said with a shrug. "The bank'll never miss it. Five hundred dollars ain't nothing to them—not the way they collect interest."

"Maybe not," Sangaree Dawson murmured, brushing his expensive hat to the back of his head, "but I sure don't like the idea of letting him get away with it."

"Can see that. It sure would help your chance of getting that United States marshal job was you to bring him in," a small, sly-faced man, also clad in a business suit and wearing a derby, observed. "It'd mean you got the bank's money back as well as catching, or killing, all four of the outlaws. Be quite a feather in your cap."

Dawson's shoulders stirred in an effort to show indifference. "Yeh, reckon it would. It ain't no secret that I want that appointment. I've paid my dues sheriffing in this state—when it was a territory and now when it's a state. I figure I've got the job coming to me."

"Not saying you ain't. What I am saying is that I need to get back to Cheyenne. I've got a business to run, and when I let you swear me in as a deputy to run down them fellows, I didn't count on being gone so long. Hell, we've been in the saddle a week and it'll take another week or so to get back. I've got to think about myself—and my business and my family."

"Goes for me, too," someone in the party added.

Another laughed. "Hell, I prob'ly ain't got no job by now," he said. "I might as well stay right here earning the dollar a day you're paying, Sheriff, as go back."

Discussion broke out among the posse members at that, all of which was ignored by Sangaree Dawson. Turning on a heel, he walked off a short distance and, halting, beckoned to Newt Thomas.

"Got something I want to say to you," he said when the deputy stood before him. "As soon the rest of the men didn't hear it."

Thomas nodded. "Sounds like most of them are getting anxious—"

"Always the way with a posse. Raring to go, all hell for leather at the start, and then right away in a hurry to get back to their wives, or whatever. How do you feel about it?"

"I'm a lawman," Thomas said quietly. "I'll do what's necessary—and what you tell me to do."

"Just what I wanted to hear from you," the sheriff said, nodding. "Want you to know that I appreciate it. What Sutton said there a bit ago about me wanting that U.S. marshal's job's the truth. I ain't ashamed to admit it."

"You've earned it, Sangaree."

"Reckon I have, but that don't guarantee me getting it—not in this day of big politics. Man has to do something special that'll draw attention to him—like me bringing down all four of them bank robbers and recovering the stolen money. Understand?"

"Sure."

"Good. Now, here's what I want you to do. I best head back to Cheyenne with the posse. Want you to stay up here and keep hunting that jasper. I expect he's running north for Montana—two maybe three days from here, according to Sutton."

Thomas nodded. "Probably what he's doing."

"Just get on the trail that's along the river and keep following it. My hunch is that it'll take you to him. When you get to the border, look around, and if you don't turn up any sign of him, then start working your way back down this direction. There's a town called Buffalo about twenty miles west of us. Wind up there. That sound all right to you?"

Newt Thomas nodded, cast a side glance at the other posse members—some squatting on their heels, others lounging against their horses.

"You know what the fellow looks like?" Dawson continued.

"Never saw him. They'd all gone and it was all over when I got to the bank."

"Well, the clerk did—he got a real good look at him as well as the others. Said he was about twenty-five, looked like a cowhand. Was wearing tan pants, a red shirt, a blue neckerchief, and a tan, flat creased hat. Got dark hair, dark eyes, mustache. Horse he rode off on was a bay."

Thomas wagged his head. "That bank clerk sure took a good look at him."

"Lucky for us," the sheriff agreed, "because ain't nobody identified any of them by name yet. Now, you bring that jasper back, dead or alive, or even proof that you brought him down, and I'll recommend you for my job—see to it that you get it, in fact."

Thomas smiled dryly. "That's if you get the appointment to be the U.S. marshal."

"Don't worry none about that. More or less had it understood with Carlton, the bank president, and the mayor before I left that they'd go to bat for me with the senator if I settle this bank holdup thing—and you know where they stand with the senator. Have we got a deal?"

The deputy smiled. "Might say that makes it a sure thing. Yeh, we've got a deal, but making one ain't necessary. I sure would like wearing your star, but laying this outlaw by the heels is not any condition to getting it. I figure it's my job. I'll go after him and bring him in whether I get your job for doing it or not."

Sangaree Dawson studied the deputy for several long moments and then shook his head. "Them's mighty high-sounding words, son, but in this here dog-eat-dog world you ain't likely to get very far feeling that way. Man's got to play the angles, pull all the strings he can—but that ain't neither here nor there. We've got a deal. You hold up your end of it, and I'll see you get what you want. Understood?"

"Understood," Thomas said, glancing toward the dead outlaws. "What do you aim to do with the dead men? Sure wouldn't want to be around if you're toting them all the way back to Cheyenne."

"Don't aim to. I'll be taking them to that town I mentioned, Buffalo, have a talk with the law there. Could be there's a wanted dodger on them. You didn't come across any writing of any kind when you was searching them, did you?"

"Nope. Nothing. And they were both flat busted, not a copper on them."

"Well, I expect the sheriff in Buffalo will have some information on them if they're wanted somewhere. Either way I'll have him give me a receipt of some kind and then bury them there. You got grub enough to last a while?"

"Starting to run short—"

"Guess we all are, but I'll tell the boys to turn over everything they've got to you so's you won't have to ride over to Buffalo to stock up. That'd cost you too much time. Me and the boys can fill our grub sacks for the ride home while we're there. I don't figure—"

"Sheriff, what do you want us to do with these here stiffs—plant them where they're laying?"

Dawson faced the posse. "We're taking them into Buffalo. Hang them across their saddles. Town ain't far from here."

"Eighteen, maybe twenty miles," the man named Sutton said. "You turning them over to the law there?"

"Figure to find out who they are, then get them buried."

"Well, now, Sheriff, we was all hoping there'd

be a reward on them that we could split up between us."

"If there is, you're welcome to it," Dawson replied with an indifferent wave of his hand. "Load them up. I want to get to that town before dark. First off, I want you to turn over what grub you've got to Thomas. He's going on."

"What about us? How'll—"

"We'll lay in a supply when we get to Buffalo."

"Now, Sheriff, I ain't fixed to do that. I come off without much cash and—"

"Don't fret about it, Carney. The county'll pay for what we need. I'll write a draft to cover what we spend."

Dawson shook his head, swore angrily under his breath. "Damned posses! I'd rather go pick droppings with the chickens than put up with one. Always so danged afraid they'll spend some of their own money. . . . You can pull out anytime you please, Deputy. No reason to hang around here."

"No reason—and I will soon as I collect the grub."

Dawson turned to the posse, now laying the bodies of the two outlaws across their saddles and securing them with rope.

"Harper, take the grub sack off Thomas' horse and put all the eating stuff the rest of the posse's carrying into it."

Harper, a squat, bandy-legged man wearing an oversized hat, immediately turned and hurried toward the deputy's horse.

"Yessir, Sheriff—"

"Think I best warn you," Dawson said, putting his attention again on Newt Thomas. "There's some kind of trouble going on up here in Johnson County. Range war, seems. You keep that star of yours out in plain sight all the time and don't put no trust in anybody till you're lead-pipe sure of them. Hear?"

"Sure do—"

"Now, if anything turns up in Cheyenne— information on this bird you're hunting, a name or something—I'll send a letter to you in care of the sheriff in Buffalo. You be sure and stop by and talk with him when you double back."

"If I haven't already got our man in chains. If I do, I'll be riding straight for Cheyenne," Thomas said, and turned to give Harper a hand with the grub.

3

Deep in nearby brush Dave Gunnison was not close enough to hear all that was being said by the sheriff, his deputy, and the other posse members, but he was able to piece together enough of the lawmen's conversation to know what lay ahead.

Newt Thomas, the deputy, was to continue north on the trail paralleling Powder River in an extended search for him. Thomas was to keep riding until he reached the Montana border; then, if unsuccessful, he was to work his way back down to the Wyoming town of Buffalo, some twenty miles west of where they presently were.

The sheriff himself was taking the bodies of Luke Redfern and Hardrock Madden on into Buffalo, where he intended to have them buried. While he was there, he also intended to have them looked up, see if there was a price on their heads. Then, after stocking up on trail grub, he'd head back to Cheyenne with the posse.

Dave had listened tensely to the two lawmen and watched as the other posse members hung the bodies of his two partners across the saddles of their horses and prepared to take them into the town. At least the sheriff whose name was Sangaree something was going to give Luke and Hardrock a decent burial. As far as wanted posters were concerned, there might be something on Hardrock, who'd run afoul of the law sometime in the past. But Madden had never talked about it, so Dave had no idea what it was. They'd find nothing on Charlie Watson, Luke Redfern, and him; up to the time they tried robbing the bank they were guilty of nothing more than knocking about the country having a good time.

"Reckon we're ready, Sheriff," one of the posse members called to Dawson. "Sutton says we're to head due west."

"Light out, then," the lawman replied, turning to his horse. As the posse mounted, he hesitated, threw a glance at Newt Thomas. "You all set to move out, Deputy?"

"I'm on my way," Thomas said, and swung up into his saddle. "See you in Cheyenne."

"Good luck," the sheriff answered, and mounting the big chestnut he was riding, angled off after the posse.

For a long ten minutes Dave Gunnison remained in the brush where he had hidden himself. Everything had blown sky-high for him. His three friends were dead, and he was now a hunted man, an outlaw—one likely to be shot on sight if recognized, judging by the treatment accorded Hardrock and Luke Madden.

But he couldn't just give up, call it quits, and turn himself in to some lawman, for he'd likely fare no better. He would have to go on. True, it would now be a different way of life. Instead of the old easy, carefree way, he was now a man on the dodge, one forever looking over his shoulder and suspicious of every dark shadow. Hell, Redfern and Hardrock and Charlie Watson just could be better off than he was! They at least had no need to be always on the run while on the lookout for some lawman eager to make a name for himself.

Moving forward to the edge of the brush, Dave turned his attention to the trail along the river. Deputy Thomas was no longer in sight. He glanced then to the west and what he could see of the road. The posse was no longer to be seen either, swallowed up by the short hills and brush.

Dropping back to where he had left his horse, Dave took up the lines and led the bay out into the clearing. Heading north up Powder River for Montana—and on to Canada—was out of the question now that Newt Thomas was blocking that route. The deputy, hungry to earn the star the sheriff was wearing, would be keeping a sharp eye not only on the trail ahead of him but behind and to the sides as well.

He had two choices, Dave concluded: he could head back south, more or less the way he'd come and try to make it into Colorado or Kansas, or he could ride on into Wyoming, taking a northwest course. Dave wasn't sure just where that would take him, but that would be working away from Deputy Newton Thomas, as well as the sheriff and the posse. He had to put as much distance between himself and the Cheyenne lawmen as possible.

Swinging up into the saddle, Dave forded the river and struck a northwesterly course. The air was cool and fresh, birds flitting in and out of the brush and singing in the cottonwood trees. Late in the morning he shot another rabbit and, halting in a shaded coulee, built a fire, skinned and roasted the small animal. He had only one biscuit left, hard as rock, and was entirely out of other food, but he still had a handful or so of coffee and, using a bit of the water from his canteen, boiled up a weak brew.

His hunger satisfied to some extent, Dave added what was left of the rabbit to that which he had in his saddlebags, tramped out the fire, and mounting, rode on. He was reluctant to stop at any ranch or homestead, knowing it would be unwise to leave any trail that Newt Thomas—unsuccessful along the Montana border and now prowling the area where Madden and Redfern had been located—might find. But he knew he'd have to do something about getting food; he couldn't go on indefinitely depending on roasted rabbit and watery coffee.

He camped that night along a small creek, ate the remainder of the two rabbits, and had another cup of coffee—this one made from the grounds he'd used earlier in the day. Near dark he saw a grouse, or perhaps it was a sage hen, perched on a log some distance away. He attempted to get near enough for a head shot but failed as the bird abruptly disappeared just when he reached an accurate shooting distance.

The night was cold and clear and passed without incident. The next morning, stiff and shivering despite his poncho and blanket, he made a fire and once again made himself coffee, fortifying the used grounds this time with a bit of fresh. The splash of a fish in the nearby creek caught his attention. He hadn't thought of satisfying his diet from that source, and hurrying down to the shallow stream, he located movement in a small backwater pool.

Moving slowly and carefully, he stepped into the cold water and with both hands scooped the fish out onto the bank. Quickly retrieving the foot-long bit of flopping, flashing silver from the grass and leaves, Dave carried it back to camp. It was a fine trout, and he lost no time in broiling and eating it.

The meal, frugal as it was, made him feel much better; he mounted up and resumed his northwesterly journey, keeping the creek in sight as he did so. He would again have fish that night for supper if he failed to find another rabbit or game of some sort.

He had no luck, although he once heard ducks quacking somewhere along the stream. His attempt to locate them failed, and he turned again to the creek, hoping to find another trout. But that, too, proved fruitless, and when he finally rolled up in his blanket and tarp, he did so with only a cup of thin coffee and some leftover rabbit under his belt. The matter of food was becoming serious, Dave realized as he lay quietly staring up into the star-bright sky. Not that he feared actual starvation; he could always eventually scare up a rabbit, a squirrel, or perhaps a grouse, and there were deer and antelope in the area, he recalled Hardrock Madden saying; he reckoned he could set himself to hunting one of the larger animals, which seemed a likely possibility now.

Whatever, he'd manage. It was not the first

time he'd known hunger, and likely it would not be the last. Sooner or later he was bound to come upon a homestead or ranch where the owner would willingly trade a square meal or two for work, but such would pose a question: should he risk showing himself and perhaps leave a trail for Newt Thomas or some other lawman to follow?

Luck was with him early that next morning when a cottontail feasting on grass off to the side of the trail offered an easy shot, presenting him with a late breakfast. He topped off the meal with another cup of weak coffee and then noticed a trickle of smoke rising up into the sky to the west. He rode on, all the while debating with himself the advisability of seeking out the source of the smoke. It would be a ranch or a homestead, and either could mean a full belly and trail grub—or eventually jail.

Around noon he broke out of the trees and other growth and halted on the rim of a vast stretch of open country. Cattle were grazing on the gray-green plain a mile or so to his right, but there was no sign of a homestead or ranch anywhere; whichever undoubtedly lay beyond a roll of land a half-mile or so on ahead. He could see trees along the rise and the smoke appeared to be lifting from the yonder side of them.

Urging the bay, who had fared well on the plentiful grass and water since the camp along the Powder River, into a lope, Dave rode across the wide flat and topped out the low ridge, eyes reaching ahead for a sign of habitation.

Abruptly a rifle shot shattered the morning quiet. Dirt flew up in front of the bay, causing it to shy violently. Cursing, Gunnison drew the horse up short and looked about for the source of the shot.

An elderly man, weapon poised in his arms, finger ready on the trigger for a second shot, sat on his horse at the edge of a small cluster of trees and was considering him coldly.

4

"Where the hell you think you're going?"

At the question Dave settled back in his saddle. The bay had quieted and his own anger had lessened somewhat.

"No place special. Riding through, mostly."

"Expect that's a lie. You're another one of the Major's hired guns."

Dave bristled. "Not lying—and I never heard of this Major."

"Ain't about to believe that either. The whole damn country's crawling with strangers—renegades he's hired to shoot and kill and burn down decent folk's property."

"Not me," Dave declared flatly. "Like I said, I'm just riding through."

The older man, somewhere in his late fifties, sat high in the saddle of the gray he was riding. Powerfully built from the years of hard life that came with homesteading, he had a rugged, weather-beaten face, dark, narrow eyes, and a full black mustache. He wore a patched, blue wool shirt, faded cord pants, and his flat-heeled boots were caked with mud.

"You claim you don't know the Major. How about a range detective called Clanton?" he asked, gaze unwavering.

"Never heard of him either. Hell, friend, I sure ain't looking for trouble. Was hoping to find a homestead or a ranch where I could trade a little work for a square meal or two and some grub, but I reckon I've come to the wrong place. Now, if you'll lower that rifle, I'll move on, get off your land."

The homesteader—or rancher—didn't stir, simply stared as he kept the weapon leveled at Dave. On beyond the man, in the deep swale well below the rise, Gunnison could see a pitched-roof house with several outbuildings, while a ditch bringing water in from a spring or stream somewhere among the trees to the west cut a narrow slash across the intervening green flat. There were fields below, and he could see chickens moving about in their wire-fenced yard, hogs in a pen, and a cow standing half in and half out of a shed. Several horses were visible in one of the corrals, and a wagon stood on the hardpack fronting the barn. Judging from the cattle he had noted, Dave reckoned the man was a combination rancher and homesteader—a union he recalled that wasn't ordinarily looked upon by either faction with favor.

"You got a name?"

"Dave Gunnison."

"Where'd you say you hailed from?"

"Never said, but Texas mostly—along with New Mexico, Kansas, Colorado, and a few other places. Mind telling me who you are?"

"Nathan King. You've been on my land for maybe the last hour or so." King's manner had softened somewhat and he seemed inclined now to be more reasonable. "You say you was just passing through?"

Dave nodded. "Right. What's all this about hired guns, and who's the Major and that range detective?" He had overheard something about the trouble in the area when he was listening to the Cheyenne sheriff and Newt Thomas talk, but it had been only scraps.

"Them two—they work for the cattle growers. Somebody got the idea that us homesteaders and small ranchers were rustling their cattle, and hired them along with a hundred other hard cases to drive us out of the country."

Dave stirred, pulled his hat lower against the slight wind that was blowing. "Can see why you're jumpy."

"I figured you were one of them, although I'll admit they usually run in bunches—six or eight, maybe ten in a party."

"They done much damage?"

"Plenty. Been several houses burned down and some killings. They call themselves Regulators. . . . You ain't heard of the hell going on up here? Folks are calling it the Johnson County War."

"No, this here's my first time in Wyoming."

"Well, if you come sight-seeing you sure picked the wrong time."

"That's for damn sure."

King looked down at his rifle, now laid across his knees. Then, brushing his misshapen, flat-crowned hat to the back of his head, he scrubbed at the stubble on his chin. "The law after you?"

Dave grinned at the directness of the question. "Yeh, reckon you can say it is."

"For a killing?"

"No. Me and three others tried to hold up a bank. Didn't work out."

"Where are the others?"

Gunnison was silent for a long breath. Then, "Dead."

King shook his head. "Expect they got what they had coming. I don't hold with breaking the law, and when a man does, he best figure on paying up for it sooner or later.... You set on riding on?"

"Well, it ain't something I've got to do. Could use a few days' work, like I said."

King reset his hat and looked out over the grassy plain. "Happens I'm a mite short on help and could use a man. Fact is, there ain't nobody on my place right now but my wife and two hired hands. Others I had took off, thanks to them dang Regulators." King paused, studied Dave thoughtfully. "Having them skulking around looking to throw a shot at you—does that make any difference?"

Gunnison shrugged. "Can't say as I like the idea of being shot at, but I reckon I can look out for myself if I have to."

"Then you can figure yourself hired."

"Think I best ask doing what?" Dave broke in. "I don't much cotton to the idea of being a hired gun."

"Won't be none of that other'n protecting yourself and my herd—and the place itself, if they take it on themselves to burn us out. I'd expect you to help me and the others drive them off."

"I'd figure on that being part of the job."

King nodded and, his rifle still across his knees, dug his heels into the gray's flanks and started the horse moving forward.

"All right then, come on. I'll take you down to the place, nod you to Jubal Phillips, he's one of the two men that had sand enough to keep working for me. Other'n is Dutch Hollister. Can meet him later. Jubal'll show you where you can bunk and fill you in on what's what around here."

Dave signified his understanding and swung his horse in beside Nathan King's.

"Now, I ain't paying much—thirty a month and food," the rancher said. "Best I can do. Things ain't been the same around here since the big blizzard, so if that ain't to your liking—"

"Suits me," Dave said, and then added, "You can oblige me plenty in one more thing."

"What's that?" King asked as the horses worked their way slowly down the slope.

"Keep it under your hat why I'm up here and where I'm from. Don't mind you saying my name— the law don't even know it. They're looking for me blind."

"Expect they've got a description of you."

"Yeh, a good one, but if I keep out of sight of a deputy who's trailing me, I figure I can slip by."

"I see. All right. All I know about you is your name. Be no sweat there. Like I said, Wyoming's overrun with strangers—some good, some bad. You got any idea where the deputy that's tracking you is now?"

"Last I saw of him he was following the Powder River north to Montana. Thinks I aimed to go there, which me and my friends planned to do. Changed my idea when I saw him head up that way."

King shrugged. "Well, you won't be bothered by him for a spell—and if he comes poking around here asking questions, he won't learn nothing."

King fell silent after that, and they continued on down the grade toward the ranch buildings. The house was a much better structure than he had thought, Dave realized when they drew near. Not of the usual sod or log construction, it was built of close fitting double-notched timbers. The glass windows had wooden shutters, and the door visible to him was a heavy plank affair with a small port in its upper section for outside viewing.

The other structures—a barn, several sheds, a roofed shelter under which a red wheeled buggy was standing—were similarly well constructed, although not of the thick timber that had been used for the main house. Dave had a closer look at the surrounding area, too, as they came into the yard. The fields to the south of the place had yet to be plowed and planted, and the small garden that he guessed supplied the Kings and their employees with fresh vegetables was also neglected.

"Sure a fine place," Dave said as they rode across the hardpack. "Can see you're needing help, all right. Shame a man has to let his place go."

Nathan King smiled tightly as they drew to a stop at the hitch rack fronting the bunkhouse.

Swinging down, he fixed Dave with a hard, steady look. "It's mine. I put my life's blood into building it up and making it what it is—and if them Regulators think they're going to burn me out, they'll have to kill me first."

Deputy Newt Thomas raised his hand and signaled for the stagecoach rolling briskly toward him to stop. He had reached the Montana border, a point indicated by a small pyramid of stones, and had turned west toward a spiral of smoke twisting up into the sky.

"What's the trouble?" The jehu called down from his perch. There were two passengers inside the coach; drummers, the deputy assumed, judging from their derby hats and checked suits.

"No trouble," Thomas replied, twisting about on his saddle so that the star he wore was more visible to the driver. "I'm looking for a man on a bay horse. I figure he came this way."

"Ain't seen nobody. What's he look like and what's his name?"

"Don't know what he's called," the deputy said, and gave the description of the outlaw he was hunting.

The driver, sharp, weather-beaten face thrust forward as if defying the continuous Wyoming wind, shook his head. "Nope, sure ain't seen nobody like that. You for certain he came this way?"

"Not much certain of anything. Just figured he followed the Powder River trail north from where he was last seen."

The driver shifted the cud of chewing tobacco in his mouth from one cheek to the other. "This is mighty big country, Deputy, and following the Powder River ain't much to go on. He could've peeled off anywheres along the way or he could've kept right on going for Canada."

"Could have, all right, but I don't think he was fixed to do much traveling. He'd be needing grub."

"They's several ranches and some homesteaders scattered around. If you've got aplenty of time you could ask them."

"Time's no big problem," Thomas said, shifting in his saddle. He'd scarcely been off the buckskin in the past twenty-four hours. "Point is, I have to run him down. Want him for trying to rob a bank in Cheyenne."

"Trying?"

"Yeh, him and three others. They're dead."

The driver hawked, spat into the dust alongside the narrow roadway. "Looks like it sure don't pay to try stealing from a bank. Well, I got to get moving. Sure sorry I can't help you none."

"Obliged to you anyway. . . . That a town on ahead where I see smoke?"

"Yeh, folks call it Goose Creek. Ain't much there any more, but if your man come up the trail, that'll likely be where he went first."

"Probably," the deputy said, and touching the brim of his gray hat with a forefinger, he rode on.

The driver of the stagecoach was right; if the outlaw he was trailing did ride north along the Powder River—something that Thomas was not fully convinced of, as he'd seen no signs of such— he undoubtedly would head for the settlement. Goose Creek, the jehu had said they called it. He'd go there and ask a few questions. If it looked as if the outlaw had not been around, then that would be sufficient proof that he'd not come up that way at all, and the best thing to do would be to turn around and head back. The man he wanted would still be in Wyoming—most likely in the area around the town of Buffalo, where his two partners had been.

5

"You'll bunk in here with Jubal and Dutch," King said, jerking a thumb at the door of the slant-roofed structure. "Corral's out back. Take your pick of the horses out there if you don't want to ride your own." The rancher stepped up onto the small landing fronting the bunkhouse and pushed open the door. "Come on—I'll tell Jubal who you are."

Ground-reining the bay, Dave followed King into the crew's quarters, a square room with built-in bunks lining its sides, a potbellied stove, and two or three chairs. Clothing hung from pegs on one wall, and the place was heavy with the smell of sweat, boots, and leather. A squat, husky man somewhere in his sixties, bearded, mustached, and with a howdy-friend kind of smile on his craggy face, turned to meet them.

"Jubal," King said, "want you to meet Dave Gunnison. He'll be working here from now on."

Phillips thrust out a gnarled hand. "Mighty glad to meet you, Dave. You're sure welcome because we're a mite short of help around here right now."

39

Gunnison took Phillips' hand into his own in a firm grasp, noting as he did the worn Colt .45 hanging on the man's hip. Jubal was a bit old to be shouldering the kind of trouble that was plaguing Wyoming's Johnson County, but as the man said who put together the first six-shooter, the weapon made its user the equal of any other regardless of size or age.

"Jubal'll tell you all you need to know about working and sleeping. You can meet Dutch when he comes in off the range," King said, and wheeling, left the room.

Phillips grinned, brushed at his beard. "Just pick yourself out any of them bunks 'cepting that'n there under the window—it's mine—or the one in the corner, it's Dutch's. Your gear out on your horse?"

Dave nodded, and while Jubal held the door open, he brought in his blanket roll, saddlebags, rifle, and other loose gear. After that, he unsaddled and removed the bridle from the bay, hung them on the top rail of the corral, and turned the horse into the enclosure. Dropping back to the bunkhouse, he entered and, bone-weary from riding, sat down in one of the ancient scarred rocking chairs. There was a low fire in the stove, and the coffeepot placed on its top surface was murmuring softly.

"You want a little Arbuckles?" Jubal asked, using the term for coffee that Dave hadn't heard in some time. "There's some ready. Maybe it won't be real hot, but I reckon it'll be strong enough to suit you."

Dave rose, crossed to his bunk, and dug his cup out of his saddlebags. Sitting back down, he held the tin container while Jubal filled it to the brim with dark, warm liquid.

"Mighty good," he said after taking a swallow. Glancing toward the window, he nodded in its direction. "What time's supper around here? Sort of late, and I don't see any smoke coming from the cook shack."

"And you won't," Jubal said. Taking a dingy-looking gray shirt off a peg at the end of his bunk, he drew it on. "Since there ain't been much of a crew around here for nigh onto a year, Nathan has us eat in the house with him and his missus. She does the cooking."

"When'll that be—supper, I mean?"

"About dark. You real hungry?"

"Some," Gunnison replied, settling back in the old rocker. "But I reckon I can hold out till then. . . . How big a herd is King running?"

"Call him Nathan," Jubal said, methodically buttoning the shirt. "Everybody does. Right now he's got about four hundred head. Lost plenty during the big blizzard a few years back."

"Shouldn't be hard for three men to handle that many cows."

"Sure wouldn't if that was all the problem we've had. Plenty of other things."

"Sort of gathered that. Nathan took a shot at me back up on the ridge east of here. Got the idea that strangers weren't exactly welcome."

Jubal wagged his head, finished dressing, and sank into one of the chairs. "That's the way it's been around here. Everybody's touchy as all get out. A man doesn't know who his friends are—and the country's full of trigger-happy galoots that as soon shoot you as take a deep breath."

"Nathan was telling me something about the trouble up here—not a whole lot but enough to know you've got a war of some kind going on."

"You went ahead and signed on to work for Nathan knowing that?"

"Yeh, reckon I did. Sure not anxious to get mixed up in a shooting match—told him so. All I was looking for when he stopped me was a couple of days work so's I could fill my belly and my grub sack, then I'd be ready to move on—told him that, too."

"Just about made up my mind to do that very thing," Jubal said, drawing a blackened pipe and a pouch of tobacco from the pocket of a red wool jacket also hanging from a peg on the wall.

Dipping the pipe bowl into the pouch, he filled it with brown shreds, stamped them down with a finger, and then firing a match with his thumbnail, puffed the well-used briar into life.

"It ain't that I'm scared," he said, blowing a cloud of smoke into the motionless air of the room. "Hell, some saddle-warmer took a shot at me only yesterday. Missed, but not by very dang much! It's just that I ain't hankering to cash in my chips yet."

"How long've you been working for Nathan?"

"Six years, more or less. He's a good, fair man, but there's a few places I want to see before I start shoveling coal for the devil."

"The hills all look alike once you been riding through them," Dave said, drinking the last of his coffee. "Take it from me. I've been chasing rainbows across this country for most of my life— since I was fifteen, in fact. Still doing it, I reckon."

"Just what I'm talking about. A man ought to

see what the rest of the country's like before he hangs up his spurs—and nobody can tell him no different. He's plain got to find out for himself."

"Expect you're right, Jubal," Dave said, pouring himself a second cup of coffee. "But don't figure to end up with nothing more than calluses on your seat and an empty belly. Nobody pays a man for drifting."

Jubal puffed thoughtfully on his pipe. "You're right, I ain't doubting that, and at my age, I reckon I ought to have better sense. Sorry thing is I ain't. . . . You worked cattle much?"

"Off and on all my life. Mostly when I was short of trail grub or some cardsharp had plucked me clean. Don't think I ever worked for a man more than one month, however."

"Nathan know that, too?"

"Expect he figured it out."

Jubal paused in his puffing to scrub at the whiskers on his chin. "Sort of surprised he'd take you on knowing that, but I reckon with things so bad, he's willing to hire anybody that come along."

Dave smiled. Jubal Phillips didn't know half the story! He was an outlaw on the run with a lawman dogging his heels, and the fact had meant nothing to Nathan King. Such was an indication, he reckoned, of how badly the rancher-home-steader needed hired hands.

"How big a crew did King have at the start?" Dave wondered, glancing about at the several bunks, now empty and covered with dust. "He must have had a pretty fair spread at one time."

"Was six cowhands at one time along with a wrangler, a couple of Indians, a Canuck that took care of the fields and the garden, and a cook. You can see what it has dropped down to: Nathan; three hands, counting you; and his missus doing the cooking. I'll tell you it was a mighty fine place to work and going good before the big blizzard hit."

"Sounds like this blizzard you keep mentioning is to blame for plenty."

"Can bet on it! We wouldn't be having all this trouble up here in Johnson County if it hadn't been for it."

Dave whistled softly. "Must have been one hell of a blow—a real humdinger."

Jubal's pipe had gone out, and knocking the ashes and dottle from it into the palm of his hand, he tossed them into a bucket half-filled with sand near the front of his bunk. In the corral behind the bunkhouse one of the horses set up a disturbance, frightened momentarily by some small animal, no doubt, or perhaps one of the countless crows that were hanging around the yard.

"Humdinger ain't exactly the right word," the old puncher said quietly. "Killer is what any of us that went through it would say—and I'll tell you why."

6

"Was the winter of '86 and '87. I recollect it real good," Jubal Phillips said, refilling his pipe. "Nathan had a couple of Indians working here on the place at the time—Crees they was. One was called Joe Moose."

Jubal paused again to light his pipe and then leaned back. "Well, Joe come in one day and said he was leaving, that he was going home. There was bad times coming, he said when I asked him why he was quitting. He'd seen several white owls, and that was a powerful bad sign. On top of that, the geese and ducks were heading south mighty early. I reckon we should have listened to old Joe, but this here's cold country and we sort of laughed it off. We'd seen bad winters before. Guess you could tell that from the way Nathan built his house and this here bunkhouse and the barn. Walls are good and thick so's they'll keep out the cold. But this winter I'm talking about was different.

"Anyway, the Crees left and we done all the things we usually done to get ready for cold weather. But we sort of noticed a change. The days got real quiet, like it usually is just before first light, and the air was kind of funny. Snow started falling early—in November—and along with it come a northwest wind. It got down below zero right quick."

"How much snow did you get?" Dave asked. The smoke from Jubal's pipe smelled good and made him long for a cigar, but he'd been broke for so long and unable to buy even a sack of Bull Durham that he'd almost cured himself of smoking.

"We got eight, maybe ten inches around here. Was deeper in other places, but it wasn't too bad. We kind of take storms like that one and keep going without no big problems. The trouble was it was only the beginning. About a month later we got another one and the snow began to pile up everywhere.

"And then came January. Along about the middle a blizzard hit us, and we had us ten days of high wind and snow. It got down to fifty below, but that was just a starter, or maybe I ought to say, a warning. The big storm some folks call the Great Blizzard come roaring in just about the time the month was over, and I'm here to tell you there ain't never been nothing like it—not before or since.

"For near four days it snowed steady while the wind—it was sharp as a knife—howled like it was coming straight out of hell. Nobody could move or go anywhere, and them folks unlucky enough to have got caught out on the range froze to death. Cattle died by the hundreds—later we found a lot of them just standing up, dead, froze stiff.

"In some of the gulches and coulees the snow had drifted and piled up to where it was ten or maybe twenty feet deep. Heard there were some places where it was a hundred. Hell, it even covered clean over a few houses."

"How many cows did you lose?"

"About three hundred, Nathan finally figured. Over the country everybody lost. The big ranchers got hit just as hard as the little ones. Somebody told Nathan the tally of dead cattle was over a million dead, counting the losses in Montana and the Dakotas.

"Was a terrible sight. Me and the rest of the crew got out soon as we could get through the drifts. Found steers everywhere—some up against a fence, some down in a coulee, some just standing out on the flats or in the creek that had froze over. We dug out all we could that were still alive, and it looked like we were going to save a fair number. Then the wind changed, blew in real warm, and melted a lot of the snow and ice. Hardly got used to that when all of a sudden the wind changed again. It got colder'n hell again, and everything froze over.

"We had a fair supply of hay in the barn, so we started feeding all the stock—ice covered all the grass so the animals couldn't graze—that we could drive in and corral. Carried fodder out to them that couldn't get through the drifts."

"Seems I remember hearing something about the blizzard you had, now that I think on it. Was down in New Mexico, or maybe it was Arizona at the time," Dave Gunnison said. "Must've been mighty hard on the ranchers losing all that stock."

Jubal nodded and, removing his pipe from his mouth, stared at it moodily. "Yeh, for a fact. We sure earned our money that winter and spring. I recollect wearing three pairs of pants, three, maybe four shirts, winding strips of wool around my feet, same around my head, and practically living in that old wool mackinaw hanging up there for days on end. Was something a man don't forget—stumbling around in snow up to his shoulders, maybe falling into a gully where it was over his head. And riding a horse was something you couldn't do. You'd climb aboard—your saddle'd be like a piece of ice—and start out. Next thing you'd be fighting to get your animal out of a drift and hoping you'd be able to do it.

"The blizzard wiped out most of the small ranchers and finished off a lot of homesteaders. They was really hard hit. If they happened to be living in a soddy, they probably was able to pull through—if they didn't get covered over too deep. It was them poor devils in tar-paper shacks and wood shanties that died—whole families just plain froze to death.

"Weren't till March that the winter let up. We got another chinook that started the snow to melting and the creeks to running, and we were able to get out and look for any of the herd that had managed to stay alive. Was a few—not many. I'll tell you one thing for dang sure: the wolves and the coyotes and the buzzards sure filled their bellies that year. Was carcasses laying around everywhere for them to feed on.

"Not long after that, the trouble started between the big ranchers and the little ones—and the homesteaders. The cattlemen claimed the little ranchers had rustled a lot of their stock, and they faulted the homesteaders, saying they not only done a lot of rustling but caused the deaths of a lot of steers that had piled up against the squatters' barb-wire fence and froze."

"Hardly blame that on them," Dave said. "Expect a lot of cows drifted up against a bluff, too, and froze."

"The truth, but the big ranchers couldn't see nothing but their way. They've got themselves a mighty strong association and a lot of the politicians are with them hand in glove—'specially here in Johnson County. Anyways, they kept piling the blame for their losses on the little ranchers and the homesteaders that were still around. I can't say about the others, but I know damn for sure that Nathan King never rounded up a cow that wasn't his. The man's honest as the day is long. I've seen him go miles out of his way to set things right.

"Now, I ain't doubting some of the homesteaders just plain helped themselves to a beef now and then. Probably had to, so's to keep their wife and kids from starving, but the ranchers didn't take that as a good reason. They figured the homesteaders shouldn't have been there in the first place.

"A lot of the big cattle outfits went busted and pulled out, but there were plenty left, and as time went on, trouble got worse. Seems like the rule was that any man who didn't belong to the association was nothing more than a rustler. Well, a lot of small ranchers didn't belong—and of course none of the homesteaders—and that made them sort of fair game for the big ranchers."

"Then that's how the trouble up here really got started," Dave broke in, setting his cup, empty for some time, aside.

"Sure is what's at the bottom of it. The association hired a bunch of range detectives to keep an eye on things. They evidently caught a few rustlers, for there was a half a dozen or so lynchings—one of them getting strung up being a woman they called Cattle Kate. It was said she was building herself a herd by going to bed with any jasper who showed up with a steer, to pay for her favors. I don't know how much of it's true, but they lynched her along with the man she was living with.

"Things just kept getting worse and worse. The big outfits who had managed to keep going were building up their herds, but they claimed they were having a tough time doing it because of the rustling. Their range detectives hadn't helped much, so they decided to take things into their own hands.

"Hired a man they called the Major—I reckon he was once in the army—and told him to get hisself a bunch of hard cases who wouldn't be scared to clean up the county the way they wanted. He done just that—brought in about fifty gunmen from Texas and Kansas and Colorado, and wherever else he could find them."

"Who's this Clanton Nathan asked me about?"

"Used to be a sheriff. The Major hired him to be his right-hand man because he knew the county real good. They got organized just like the association wanted and started calling themselves the

Regulators. The homesteaders and small ranchers wasn't a-napping all that time. They formed themselves a sort of association, too, and put out the word that they sure wasn't going to be run off by the bunch that called themselves Regulators."

"Nathan belong?"

"Nope. Heard him tell one of them that rode out to see him a couple of days ago that he was staying clear of such. Said he had enough trouble keeping his place going without asking for more." Jubal once again cleaned his pipe and wagged his head. "Reckon that about brings you up to now. Can see what Nathan's up against—he ain't siding with either outfit."

"Sort of like walking the top rail of a corral."

"Exactly, and I sure don't like the way it's all shaping up. The Major and his Regulators are running wild all over the country, and the homesteaders and little ranchers are cocking their guns and getting ready for a showdown.

"I'm just too old and beat-up for such any more. Was a time when I'd have jumped at the chance to go packing iron, but no more. Hell, I ain't done nothing with this old hog leg of mine but drive nails for many a year."

Dave grinned. He felt the same as Jubal did: he had no taste for a range war either, although age was not his reason.

"Expect Nathan'll think I'm kind of a bunch-quitter, walking out on him like I figure to do, but truth is I'm real tired of everything. I'd just like to go somewhere and set in the sun for a spell. I don't think I've got all the cold from that blizzard out of my bones yet, and I sure—"

The sharp, clear ring of metal broke in on Jubal Phillips' words. He shrugged, tucked his pipe into a pocket of his shirt, and got to his feet. In the shadowy light inside the bunkhouse the lines of his leathery face appeared deeply etched, and his pale blue eyes were almost colorless.

"I reckon that's what you've been waiting to hear—Nathan's missus ringing the supper bell. Let's go eat."

"You don't have to tell me twice," Dave said with a grin. "Lead the way."

7

The interior of the house was comfortably if sparsely furnished, Dave saw as he followed Jubal Phillips into the structure. They passed by a wide hall off which it appeared several rooms opened, and entered the dining area that adjoined the kitchen. Nathan was already seated at the table. He motioned Dave to take the chair next to the one Phillips drew back.

"You all settled?" the rancher asked.

Dave nodded. "Ready to go to work."

A half-smile cracked King's lips. "You mind chopping and ricking wood?"

Gunnison winced noticeably. It was not a chore he favored, but he had asked for work, and if that was to be a part of the job, he reckoned he could stand it—at least for a couple of days.

"Sure not something I sit up nights hoping to do the next day," he said. "But if that's what you want, I—"

King laughed. "Glad to see you didn't back off. Ain't no man I ever hired liked to cut and split wood, but sometimes it has to be done. We're all

right now—got plenty for the missus' cookstove
and for what heating we're having to do. Later
on, howsomever, we'll be needing to lay in a
fresh supply. I've been hoping to hire somebody
in town to—"

King broke off as his wife appeared in the
doorway bringing two large platters of food—one
covered with steak, the other piled with fried
potatoes and golden-brown biscuits. Dave's eyes
centered first on the food and then switched
abruptly to the surprisingly young woman.

"This here's a new hand, Bettina," Nathan
said, gesturing at Dave. "Name's Gunnison—Dave
Gunnison. He's from down Texas way."

Dave, prompted by some long-neglected cour-
tesy, half-rose to acknowledge the introduction.

"This here's my wife Bettina, Dave."

Gunnison nodded, managed a smile, but he
was having difficulty concealing his surprise.
Bettina King could be no more than twenty or
twenty-one, he was sure, which would make Nathan around three times her age. Pretty, a shapely
figure visible despite the housedress she was wearing, Bettina had dark hair and brows, blue eyes,
and smooth, creamy tanned skin. She looked more
the rancher's young daughter than his wife.

"How do, ma'am," Dave murmured, and sank
slowly back onto his chair.

"Very well, Dave. Welcome to our ranch. . . .
I'll get the coffee and some honey for your biscuits," she added, smiling at her husband. "We'll
have pie later."

"Dried apple," King said. "I've got a half a
dozen trees in my orchard, but apples are the

only thing I've had any luck with. . . . Might as well start eating. The missus will be along in a bit."

The rancher took up his fork and speared one of the steaks and then helped himself to the potatoes and biscuits. Jubal followed suit, and Dave, needing no urging, immediately began to fill his plate.

He had yet to get over his surprise at seeing Nathan King's wife. Instead of the large matronly woman with broad florid features, heavy arms, and work-hardened hands he had expected, Bettina King had turned out to be a young beauty who would elicit a second glance from any man.

After his second steak and another helping of potatoes and several honey-filled biscuits, Dave turned then to the hot apple pie—a piece liberally spread with butter.

"I hope you'll like working for us here," he heard Bettina say. She had a light, happy-sounding voice with almost a lilt to it. "Wyoming is a fine place to live, but then I guess you know that."

"No, ma'am. It's my first time up here. I'm—"

"It *was* a fine place to live," Nathan cut in. "Can't say much for it now—not with it being overrun by killers and firebugs and the like."

"The country's still a fine place," Bettina said, smiling. "I'm not talking about the men running loose over it. Did you have any trouble today, Nathan?"

The rancher shook his head. "Seen a bunch of riders over near them buttes on the south range.

Looked to be headed for town. Gunnison here's the only one I ran into."

"Where were you going, if you don't mind my asking?" Bettina said, her attention on Dave as she picked at the last of the pie on her plate with her fork.

"No place special. Was out looking for work."

"And dang nigh got hisself shot," Nathan said, shaking his head. "These Regulators have got me jumpy as a cat in a yard full of dogs."

"Which brings up some talking I've got to do, Nathan," Jubal Phillips, quiet up to that moment, said. Eyes locked onto the cup of coffee he was holding in his two hands, he added, "I'm quitting."

"Quitting!" Bettina echoed. "I don't—" She fell silent quickly as the rancher lifted his hand to stem her words.

"I reckon that's your privilege, Jubal," he said heavily. "I'd like to know why."

"Well, it ain't that I'm liking to do it, or maybe even like myself for pulling out, but I've been thinking about it for a spell—and you've got Dave here to take my place."

"Still short-handed even putting him on."

"I know that, Nathan, and I'm right sorry about leaving, but well, I ain't got no business mixing up in a range war, and this sure as blazes is what this ruckus has turned into."

"Ain't none of us wanting that."

"I'm tired of getting shot at by some bushwhacker I can't even see. Maybe I'd feel different if it wasn't like that—it's the never knowing that gets to crawling up a man's backbone. I'm real sorry, Nathan, and I'm a-hoping you'll understand and—"

"No need running on and on about it," the rancher interrupted. "You've been with me a long time, and you're a good man."

"But a mite old now," Jubal said.

"I ain't never had cause to complain about your work," King continued. "When we're done eating, I'll get some cash and pay you off. I figure you've got about a week's wages due you."

"Can forget that. I got all the money I need, leastwise till I can find myself another job. Expect I owe you, leaving real sudden like I am."

Silence filled the room. Bettina King resumed picking at her dessert, Jubal's eyes remained fixed on the empty cup he was holding, and Nathan, downing the last of his coffee, leaned back in his chair. Out in the yard somewhere a meadowlark was whistling cheerfully.

Dave, finished with his meal, let his eyes travel about the room, bare except for the large square table, the solidly built chairs, and three or four cattle-feed-company calendar pictures on the smooth timber walls.

"How do you feel about the job now?" King asked suddenly, placing his attention on Dave. "Expect Jubal's given you the whole story about how things are around here."

"Yeh, sure has."

"Country's full of trigger-happy shooters, and if a man ain't careful, he can get hisself a bullet in the back real easy."

"Sort of figured that."

"Know my offer of thirty a month and grub ain't much for the kind of job it is, but it's all I can afford. I'm still trying to get on my feet after what that damn blizzard done to me."

"Jubal said you lost a lot of stock."

"Everybody did. That's what brought on all the hell around here—folks accusing their neighbors of rustling, homesteaders getting burned out, killing and lynching—everybody's gone looney! And worst of all, the army just looks the other way, and the law ain't able to do nothing. If you want to ride on, I won't fault you none."

Dave said nothing. He wasn't too pleased with prospects on Nathan King's combination ranch and homestead; in fact, he wasn't very happy at all about being in Wyoming. But Bettina King set a fine table and Nathan appeared to be a square and honest man, one he could work for.

"I've quit trying to beat luck," the rancher went on. "I'm just taking things as they come. If you leave, like as not another drifter'll show and maybe be hard up enough to stick around. Can do what you figure's best for you, stay or move on, just want you to know what you're up against. Supper's on me, so—"

The outer door slammed, brought Nathan's voice to a stop, and all turned toward the doorway to the hall. A slim, ruddy-faced, black-eyed, bearded cowhand somewhere in his forties, dressed in cord pants, faded army shirt, and wearing stovepipe boots, appeared in the entrance.

"Dutch," King said, a worried look pulling at his features. "Something wrong?"

"Plenty—I come in early to tell you," Hollander said. "Jesse Haines rode by a hour or so ago. He'd been in town. Said he had word for you."

"So?" King pressed, frown deepening.

"Said to tell you the Major, the head of them Regulators, has put your name on his death list."

8

A hush seized the room following Hollister's words, one that was broken only by the gasp that escaped Bettina's lips. And then Nathan's calm, deep voice broke the quiet.

"Set down, Dutch, and eat your supper. . . . Bettina, how about some hot coffee?"

Hollander dropped wearily onto one of the chairs and proceeded to help himself to the still plentiful food on the table.

"Jesse have anything else to say?" King asked when Bettina had returned and was filling Hollander's cup.

"Nope, just that—that, along with saying things are mighty upset in Buffalo. Sheriff's getting real worried about them Regulators."

"About time," King said dryly, and then nodded at Dave. "Fellow there's named Dave Gunnison, Dutch. He's maybe going to work for me."

Hollander paused for an instant in his eating as if startled by the information, but said nothing, simply nodded his welcome and resumed his meal.

"I don't see why the Major would be holding

anything against you, Nathan," Bettina said, again in her chair. "You haven't sided with either the homesteaders or the ranchers."

"Expect that's what's wrong," Jubal commented. "Seems if a man ain't for the cattle growers, then he's against them. There ain't no middle ground. You figure if you went to see the Major or sent word to him that you ain't taking no hand in the ruckus a'tall, he'd leave you alone?"

King's jaw clamped shut. "You know me better than that, Jubal. I won't crawl and I won't beg, and if he sends some of his hard cases out here after me, they'll have a fight on their hands."

"And there's plenty of them," Dutch said between sips of coffee. "Jess said the cattle growers was paying five dollars a day and expenses with a special bonus of fifty dollars for every rustler killed."

"Everybody's a rustler to their way of looking at it," King said, "and that kind of pay's bound to bring in more gunfighters. The Major ought to have himself quite an army before its done with. . . . You see anybody else on the range today, Dutch?"

Hollander, finished with the steak and potatoes he'd piled on his plate and wolfed down, was now working on a thick wedge of the pie. He nodded. "Sure did. Seen about a dozen riders over to the north. Was a bunch of them Regulators, I expect."

"They come onto my land?"

"Not so's I could tell. Lot of brush and some deep gulches along there. Now, they might have, but if they did, I couldn't see them." Dutch turned his reddish countenance to Dave. "You ever work cattle or are you a yard hand?"

"I've done my time riding fence and popping steers out of the brush. Same goes for being a yard hand," Dave said stiffly.

Hollander gave what passed as a smile, and nodded. "Wasn't meaning to upset you, was just wanting to know what me and Jubal can expect. If we're getting somebody we'll have to wet-nurse along, we're better off—"

"Jubal's riding on," King cut in. "Quitting."

A long, gusty sigh escaped Hollander's lips. "Aw, hell," he murmured, and then glancing apologetically to Bettina, said, "Why?"

"Best you let Jubal answer that."

Dutch said no more until he had finished his dessert and had taken a long swallow of coffee. Only then did he turn his attention to his old friend.

"I reckon you got your reasons for doing it, and I ain't got the right to ask you why. I'm right sorry I did. Only like I say we've been saddle partners for quite a spell, and I sure hate to see you go."

"Kind of hate to go, Dutch. This here place is the closest thing to a home I've ever had—thanks to Nathan and his missus—but I've done made up my mind."

"Expect you're aiming to put in a lot of time down at the Hog Ranch. When you get there tell all the gals howdy for me, and that I'll be around first chance I get. Other'n that, there ain't nothing else to say except good luck."

"Obliged, Dutch, and I'll pass the word along for you, but I expect we'll be doing some more talking before I ride on in the morning."

"Ain't likely," Hollander replied in his flat, positive way. "I'll either be sleeping or working. . . . Nathan, I seen a lot of smoke to the east just before I come in. You figure maybe it was them Regulators torching the Connors' place?"

"Them, or some outlaws, all right. How long ago was it you saw that bunch north of here?"

"Been three hours or so—maybe a mite less. You want me to take a ride up there and see if they're still hanging around?"

"No, you've put in your time since morning. I'll go myself."

"I'm beat sure enough, but I reckon I can still set my saddle and shoot if it becomes needful."

King shook his head. "You go on to bed. If it turns out I need help, I'll come back and roust you out."

"I'll go," Jubal Phillips volunteered.

"No," King said flatly. "You've quit. You ain't part of this ranch no more, and you can leave anytime you want."

Immediately Jubal pushed back his chair and got to his feet. Face slightly red and nodding politely to Bettina, he said, "Never been no hand to hang around where I wasn't wanted, so I reckon I'll roll up my blankets, get my war bag, and move on. Just want to say, however," he added in a more mollified tone, "I ain't got no hard feelings toward anybody. Good luck."

Dave and the others at the table murmured a like response and then listened to the thud of Jubal's heels as he left the room, and the slam of the screen door when he stepped out onto the hardpack. At that Bettina rose, made the rounds refilling coffee cups from the heat-streaked granite pot, and then once more sat down.

"Can't figure old Jubal out," Dutch said, digging into the pocket of his shirt for pipe and tobacco. "Must be something real bad that'd—"

"Said he was too old to face the trouble we're having," King said, "at least that's what it amounted to. I'm not saying he's scared, mind you, it's just that he don't want to get mixed up in it." The rancher broke off abruptly and turned to Dave.

"You heard what Jesse Haines told Dutch. What with my name on the Major's list and him hiring on more gunfighters, I reckon you could say the war is here. Told you you could ride on or you could stay. Time's come to stand up and be counted. Make your choice."

Dave took up his cup and sipped slowly at the cool coffee—good coffee, he realized, not the watered-down chicory but the real thing. He raised his glance, met Bettina King's eyes. She was studying him intently, and as he watched, the word *please* formed silently on her lips. She was hoping he'd stay, hoping he'd not ride out on her husband as Jubal Phillips had.

Gunnison dropped his gaze. He had a strong feeling that he should do as Jubal did—move on before matters got any worse. He had no heart for mixing in a range war, and he could just as easily hide from Deputy Newt Thomas elsewhere in Wyoming or Montana as in Johnson County. He'd be a fool to stay, get himself involved in a lot of shooting and killing—and maybe end up dead to be planted in some lonely flat where nothing grew but scrub grass and the only thing passing by were the coyotes and the everlasting wind.

And if he stayed and lived through it, what would he gain? A job that would pay him thirty a month and meals for riding herd on a bunch of dumb, contrary critters twelve hours a day. Sure, accommodations would be good—a warm, dry comfortable bunk to sleep in, and fine grub that beat anything he was ever able to buy in a home restaurant when he was flush. But was that enough?

He lifted his eyes again to Bettina as he took another swallow of coffee. The pleading was still in her eyes, and he thought he could detect the word *please* again on her lips.

What the hell! He'd gone hungry for the past two months; his tail was sore from riding, and Nathan King—and Bettina—needed help. If he rode on, there'd be only the rancher and Dutch Hollister to make a stand against the outlaws and the bunch that called themselves Regulators.

"Reckon I'll stick around," he said, setting his empty cup back on its saucer.

A wave of relief crossed Bettina's face and a smile parted her lips. Dutch Hollander nodded his approval.

"Fine," Nathan King said briskly, "but we best understand one thing. I won't have you changing your mind the first time a bullet notches your hat brim."

"If I sign on for a job, I stay with it."

"Pleased to hear that. I think you and me best take a ride up to the north range, see if those birds Dutch spotted earlier are still there."

"Sure thing," Dave said, getting to his feet.

"You go saddle your horse. It'll take me only a minute to get my six-gun."

"You're welcome to strap on mine," Dutch said, rising and unbuckling his belt.

The holster was filled with an early model Colt pistol, once a cap-and-ball weapon but now converted to using brass cartridges—an alteration perfected by a man named Thuer. Dave had once owned a similar gun but had lost it one night in a poker game.

"Never mind," King said, moving toward the hallway. "I'm used to mine. Best you keep your iron handy anyway, just in case trouble starts around here while we're gone."

"Sure, I savvy," Hollander said. "If you hear me shoot twice real fast, and then a third time, that'll mean for you to come a-running."

"Fine—that'll be the signal," King said, and added over his shoulder, "Dave, I'll meet you at the corral."

9

As Dave and Nathan King rode out of the yard, Gunnison could see Jubal Phillips through the dusty window of the bunkhouse getting his belongings together as he prepared to leave. Dave felt a pang of regret at the older man's departure and wished that it could be otherwise, but he understood how Jubal felt. He would have liked the chance to talk to Phillips before he left, however, and wish him luck.

"Best we swing east," King said as they left the hardpack and struck out across the open range, stirring briskly as a late-afternoon wind riffled the grass. "Lots of brush up where Dutch said he seen that bunch. Be easier to move in on them from that side."

Dave nodded and, reaching down, drew his .45. Holding it at an angle, he thumbed open the loading gate of the weapon and spun the cylinder. The gun was fully loaded and ready for use—if such became necessary.

"I reckon you've been cut in on a deal like this before," King said. His weather-beaten features were grim, and he had the look of a man tired of being patient and careful and now willing to bring matters to a head.

"Once," Dave replied.

"In Texas?"

"No, was over in Kansas a few years back. Fellow named Ward decided to take over a big chunk of land where a dozen or so squatters had settled."

"They been there long?"

"Yeh. Most of them had moved in about ten years or so earlier. Had built themselves up pretty decent farms, had nice homes and families."

"How'd it end?"

"Killings—too much of it. Just like what's going on around here. When it was over, the squatters had been driven out. Ward was just too big and strong for them."

King was silent for a long minute. Then, "Which side was you on—this Ward's or the homesteaders?"

"Ward's," Dave said. "Not proud now that I had a hand in it, but at the time it was just a job."

They rode on swinging wide in order to come in from the blind side of the brushy area where Dutch Hollander had spotted the Regulators. The wind was increasing in strength and now was whipping the larger clumps of brush back and forth, whistling as it hurried through the trees not yet leafed out.

"How do you feel about this here deal?" King asked after a time. "You're on the homesteader side of it if you stick with me."

Gunnison's wide shoulders stirred. "Like before—it's a job."

"Meaning that if the Major had got to you first, you'd probably be working for them?"

"Maybe—"

They pressed on as the sun sank lower toward the hills to the west. The wind continued, and here and there bright spots of early spring flowers were to be seen. A flock of crows straggled by overhead, and once they frightened a dozen antelope that raced off to the south, their white rumps flashing in the sunlight as they fled.

Abruptly King drew to a stop. "There's their horses," he said.

Dave had spotted the animals—three of them— at the same instant. Tied to a small tree at the edge of a line of thick brush that apparently ringed a coulee, they stood quietly with their heads down, hip slacked, a picture of weariness.

"Can move on till we get to the upper end of that sage. We'll leave the horses there and move in on them. Most likely they've hunkered down in that hollow to get out of the wind."

"What's your plan?" Dave asked. "We go in shooting or are you aiming to talk?"

"Leaving it up to them," King answered as they continued on.

They reached the large clump of silver brush, halted, and quietly dismounted. Securing their horses to the base of the shrub, they drew their guns and began to work their way toward the coulee.

"Sure was a right funny sight—yessir, it was!" The voice coming from the hollow was filled with laughter. "You should've seen them nesters. They was all out in front of their dugout when we come riding up. They took one look at us and then scattered like chickens in a hailstorm—kids and grown-ups going in every direction. I laugh every time I think about it."

Dave, standing close beside Nathan King, saw the rancher stiffen angrily and take an involuntary step forward. Reaching out, he laid a hand on the rancher's arm. They had not caught a glimpse of the men yet, and it would be foolish to move in until they knew exactly what they were up against. There could be more than three in the party of Regulators, the others having picketed their horses at the lower side of the brush.

"Wait. Best we have us a look first," he murmured.

The voice of the man in the coulee continued. "Was a couple of mighty pretty little gals in the bunch. Young. Maybe fifteen or sixteen. Me and Hedrick aim to drop back and make ourselves acquainted first chance we get—if you know what I mean."

"Sure, I know what you mean, all right, Murph, and you better watch your step. It's going to get you in trouble with the Major if you ain't careful."

"The Major? Hell, he don't care. He's been hired to drive the nesters out of the country anyway he can. That makes plump little quail like them two gals fair game for me and Hedrick—or anybody else."

Suddenly Nathan King started toward the sound of the voices—only two, Dave realized. Once again he grabbed for the rancher's arm, but King shook him off and, gun in hand, pushed forward through the brush. At once Dave followed, and a moment later they had reached the edge of the coulee and were stepping into the open.

Two men—three horses. That fact registered more fully on Dave Gunnison's mind. King didn't appear to recognize the discrepancy—or simply did not let it bother him.

"Get your hands up and keep them up," the rancher snarled. "You're trespassing on my land and I've a damned good notion to blow your heads off—knowing why you're here."

The two men—one squat and dark, with many nickel conchae decorating his leather vest; the other a medium-built individual in a dusty blue suit, derby, and wearing crossed gun belts—complied slowly.

"Who the hell are you?" the squat one demanded, no fear or hesitation in his voice.

"Name's King. This is my range."

Dave, acutely conscious of the missing man, drew off a bit to the right where he could watch at least two sides of the hollow. The third man could come in from either—or, forewarned by voices, he could make a stealthy approach through the sagebrush.

"King—yeh, your name's on the Major's list," the derby-hatted man said. "We been aiming to pay you a call, haven't we, Murph?"

The brazen attitude of the men, apparently Regulators, was surprising. Most faced with guns leveled at them and clearly in the wrong would talk softly and hope to stay the trigger of the weapons threatening them.

"I'm serving notice on you now," King said evenly, "if you or any of your outlaw crowd ever comes onto my range again, I'll kill you—every last one of you. Goes for that renegade you call the Major, too!"

"Do tell," Murph said in a sarcastic tone. "My, but you sodbusters sure can get brave sometimes—ain't that so, Gates?"

"Well, now, he ain't just a sodbuster, Murph, he's a rancher, too."

"I see. Got one of them little two-bit, ragged-ass outfits that's messing up the range for real cattlemen."

A surge of anger claimed Nathan King. His arm came up and the revolver in his hand abruptly broke the quiet of the plains country. Murph staggered back, clutching at his shoulder. The man called Gates—round, ruddy face suddenly pale—raised his hands higher.

Gunnison muttered a curse and hastily glanced about. He had wanted to locate the third man before they made any move, and be ready and waiting for him; the gunshot would have alerted the Regulator, put him on guard. What advantage they had was now lost.

"Get their guns, Dave," King said. "We'll take them over to the Connors'—expect it was them that set fire to their place—and let them hold their own hanging."

Dave, back to the densest part of the brush stand, eyes searching the area before him as he sought to catch a glimpse of the missing man, evidently named Hedrick, waited several moments while he listened and watched.

Nathan King stirred impatiently. "You hear me?"

Dave nodded. "I hear you, but there's a third

man around somewhere. Like to know where he is."

Nathan frowned. "Was three horses, all right," he said as if just remembering. "Go ahead. I'll keep my eyes peeled."

"Best thing you can do is drop that gun you're holding," a harsh voice cut in from behind Dave. "Means you, too, cowboy."

Nathan allowed his weapon to fall to the ground. Dave, frustration stirring through him, followed suit.

"Get your hands up!"

Dave raised his arms slowly, hearing the crackle and swish of brush in back of him as Hedrick shouldered his way through.

"Where the hell you been?" the man in the derby hat demanded. "Farmer there's gone and plugged Murph. He's bleeding like a stuck hog."

"Was busy—come soon as I heard that shot," Hedrick snapped, breaking out into the open. An average-sized man dressed in a faded Confederate army uniform and carrying a rifle, he advanced warily toward his two friends.

"Get over here and hold your gun on them," Gates ordered. "I got to tie a bandage around Murph's arm and try to stop the bleeding. Then we'll take care of them two hayseeds."

Hedrick quickened his step. Dave tensed. If he or Nathan didn't do something quick, they were both dead, and the rancher, standing out in the open as he was, would have little chance to act.

Eyes on Hedrick, Dave gauged his possibilities. The Regulator called Gates, assuming Hedrick had the situation in hand, had turned to his wounded partner and was tearing away the man's bloody shirt. If Hedrick would pass near enough, Dave thought, he just might be able to lunge, grab the rifle the Regulator was holding, and take it from him. And if King were watching and if he were quick enough, he could pick up his gun, and the two of them would then have things going their way again.

But it all would have to be done in the next few moments. Like as not there were more of the Major's riders close by. Others had been seen in the area, and the gunshot could draw them. Unless he and Nathan King were ready for an all-out show down with probably a dozen or more of the hired gunmen, they would have to move fast.

The opportunity Dave hoped for came unexpectedly soon—so much so that he almost missed it. Hedrick, crossing toward his partners and little more than an arm's length away, stumbled on the uneven ground. It was all Gunnison needed. Reacting, he threw himself at the man and seized the rifle Hedrick was carrying by the stock. The Regulator yelled and held tight to the weapon's barrel.

Instantly Dave changed tactics. Putting all his strength into it, he pivoted, swung Hedrick, clinging desperately to his rifle, around in a half-circle. The Regulator lost his grasp on the weapon and, stumbling, went hard into Gates and the wounded Murphy. Cursing wildly, all three went down in a tangle of flailing arms and legs.

10

"You aiming to kill them here and now?"

Dave, in possession of the rifle, bent down and picked up his pistol. King also had recovered his weapon. At the question the rancher stared at Gunnison.

"You started something—shooting that one. If they stay alive they'll be back—probably with a half-dozen more of their bunch—looking to even the score."

King shook his head. "Hell, I can't do that. It'd be cold-blooded murder."

Dave, rifle leveled at the three men struggling to regain their feet, shrugged. "When you're dealing with their kind, you have to look at it the same as they do—but you're the boss."

"We'll do like I said," King murmured, looking away. "Put them on their horses and take them over to the Connors. Let them do what they want. . . . I'll collect their guns."

Dave was silent as King began to disarm the three riders. He was not in favor of murder any more than Nathan King, but he knew there were times when a man must forgo his principles and do what was necessary. Otherwise he only created for himself and his a larger and more dangerous problem.

"Ain't far to the Connors," King said, coming back to Gunnison's side with the weapons the Regulators had been carrying. "We—"

Dave glanced over his shoulder. "Don't think we'll get a chance to take them anywhere. I've got a hunch there's more of them close by—more than we can handle."

"You're damn right about that, mister," Gates shouted, face flaming with anger. "You done bit off a hell of a lot more'n you can chew."

Dave eyed the man sardonically. "Maybe we best go ahead and shoot them now—like I suggested. It'd put an end to them—to their talking and coming back."

King, catching Gunnison's drift, nodded. "Maybe you're right. Sure be a lot less trouble."

Hedrick brushed nervously the sweat and dust on his sunburned face. "Just you hold up a minute," he shouted, suddenly anxious. "That'd be plain murder, and you sure don't want—"

"But it's all right for you to go around murdering folks," Dave cut in. "Wind blows both ways."

"What we don't want is you or anybody else in that bunch of outlaws you call Regulators coming onto my land," King said coldly. "Reckon the best way to stop it is do what you're doing—by killing."

Dave, eyes continuing to probe the area visible to him for signs of oncoming riders, and seeing none at the moment, turned his attention to King. "Whatever we're going to do we best do it real quick."

King nodded. "Get the horses. I'll decide what's best to do with them while you're gone."

Moving around the end of the brush to where the horses were tethered, Dave collected the reins and began to lead the animals back to the coulee.

"We ain't burned nobody out," he heard Hedrick say as he entered the hollow. "Wasn't us, mister. This here's the first place we come to. We only got hired on yesterday."

King studied the men for a long minute. "Maybe so, but that don't stack no hay with me. You're all working for the same man, and if you'd had the chance, you would've set fire to my place, shot my cattle, and killed me or Dave here or some of the other men working for me."

Hedrick had no answer for that, nor did the derby-hatted Gates or Murph, who was still clutching his shoulder and moaning softly. Dave had no idea now what King had in mind, but he feared the rancher would weaken, perhaps even take the three back to the ranch and have his wife tend to Murph's wound. He hoped not. It would be like cuddling up to a rattlesnake.

"Going to go easy on you," the rancher said. "We ain't taking you over to the Connors—and we won't waste lead on shooting you down. You can get on your horses and head back to wherever you're working out of."

"You mean you're letting us go?" Gates asked in a strained, almost incredulous voice.

"I am, and when you get there, you tell the Major that the next time we catch any of your bunch on my range, it won't go so easy for them. I'm giving orders to my men to shoot on sight. That clear?"

Dave swore softly under his breath. King could at least have taken the three men in and handed them over to the law in Buffalo. Such would perhaps put them out of circulation for a time, but Nathan King was calling the shots.

"It's clear," Hedrick said grudgingly.

Gates, a sly sort of humor in his eyes, nodded. "Sure, we got it straight, but this here ain't the last verse no matter what you say. Song's a long ways from being finished."

"It will be for you unless you get the hell out of here," Dave snapped impatiently, drawing his weapon. "Mr. King's giving you your hide back. Mount up and ride out."

The three men moved slowly away from the edge of the brush and to their horses.

Midway Gates looked back. "Ain't you giving us our guns?"

"No," King said flatly.

"Could shuck the shells, leave them empty. Hell, a man's half-naked without his iron."

"Forget it," King snapped. "I aim to use your guns to fort up my own place in case you or any of the rest of the Major's bunch try coming around again."

Saying no more, the three Regulators climbed onto their horses, cut about, and headed south.

King swore softly in relief. "Mighty glad we're out of that one. Would've like to take them into the sheriff and let him handle them, but I wasn't sure we'd make it—not with so damn many of them running loose. Same goes for taking them over to the Connors' place. Not even sure if there's any of the family left or that we'd ever get there with them."

Dave shrugged. "Probably a big mistake letting them go."

"What else could I've done?" King demanded, anger and impatience in his voice.

Again Dave Gunnison's shoulders stirred. "Expect you did the only thing you could. Trouble is you'll for sure have the Major's bunch on your neck now and fast. . . . What about those guns you've got? Can throw them in that wash, cover them over."

The rancher smiled. "Figure to do just what I said—tote them back to the house and have them handy if the Major's bunch ever comes at us. Come on, let's get out of here before we do have some company that won't exactly be the friendly kind."

Deputy Newton Thomas pulled up at the sagging hitch rack of the Big Horn Saloon, and stared moodily at its cracked and weathered facade. He had no idea nor did he know if it was in Wyoming or neighboring Montana. About the only thing he was certain of was that he'd found no trace of the outlaw he was searching for, and worse yet, he had no real idea where to look for him.

Sighing, leg, back, and shoulder muscles aching from the endless hours in the saddle, he swung down and wrapped the reins of the tired buckskin about the crossbar of the rack. Then brushing his hat to the back of his head, he started for the door of the Big Horn.

"Ain't nobody in there—"

At the sound of the voice coming from a few

paces away, Thomas turned. A man had appeared in the doorway of what at one time had been a livery stable.

"Place closed?"

"Sure is."

"Permanent or for now?"

"I reckon you could say permanent. Fellow that owned it's dead."

Thomas nodded, moving nearer to the man. He could see no one else among the weed-overgrown street or around the empty-looking houses, but the general store on down the way a short distance appeared to be open for business.

"You live hereabouts?"

"Sure do—twenty year. Got me some sheep."

"Good money in wool," the deputy said, and extended his hand. "My name's Thomas. I'm a deputy sheriff from Cheyenne."

"Long way," the man commented, accepting the lawman's hand. "I'm Henry Morland."

"Pleased to meet you. I'm looking for a man who was in on a bank robbery. Think he came this way."

"Figured it was something like that," Morland said. "He got a name?"

"Expect he has, but I don't know what it is," Thomas said, and gave his description of the wanted outlaw.

When he was finished, Morland shook his head. "Ain't seen nobody like that around here. You sure he was headed this way?"

"Up the Powder River trail, we thought," the deputy said with a shrug. Suspicion had been growing within him since early that morning that he was on the wrong track, that the bank robber

had not headed north at all—at least not along
the Powder River. There'd been no sign along
the trail, no fresh hoof prints, no ashes from a
recent fire, and no glimpse of a rider on the
distant horizon. And now this. The outlaw would
have sought out the first town he could find
since he unquestionably was short of grub. Thomas
turned back to Morland.

"There a chance this renegade could have come
here and you din't see him?"

Morland, a leathery man with dark, squinting
eyes, wearing overalls, a wool shirt, and a sheep-
skin coat to ward off the cold wind that swept
across the grasslands, pulled off his ragged-
brimmed hat and fixed his gaze on the irregular,
gray-blue mass to the west that was the Big Horn
Mountains.

"Ain't never nothing for certain," the sheep
man said. "Why don't you just go on over and
have yourself a talk with John Allwood at the
general store. Maybe he can help you, seeing as
how I can't."

Thomas smiled at the faint edge to Morland's
tone. "Be a good idea. I'm obliged to you," he
said, and dropping back to the buckskin, mounted
and rode the short distance to the store—a rock
and tin-roofed affair standing slightly apart from
the other decaying structures.

Allwood was alone in the store, which apparently had but a limited clientele, judging from
the small stock on the dusty shelves. Thomas
introduced himself and made known his purpose.
The squat, ruddy-faced storekeeper, wearing
denim pants and a shirt with Indian beadwork
on it, gave an immediate reply.

"No, sure ain't been nobody like that in here. Ain't been no strangers through here in weeks, excepting them riding the stage, and they don't stop unless they're needing something. What're you after this fellow for?"

"Was in on a bank robbery down in Cheyenne— him and three other men. We got all of them but him."

Allwood took a snuffbox from a pocket, tucked the tobacco powder into the space between gums and a cheek. "Well, I sure ain't seen him, and I doubt he went east. Nothing that direction, and real mean traveling. Like as not, he was needing grub if he left Cheyenne in a big rush."

Newton Thomas nodded. "He did. I'm beginning to think I've had a long ride for nothing. . . . But speaking of grub, there's a few things I'm getting low on."

"Just you name them," Allwood said cheerfully. "What I'm here for."

"Salt, couple tins of biscuits, half side of bacon—"

"Got salt pork, no bacon."

"All right, salt pork. Need some beans, spuds, and about ten pounds of grain for my horse."

"Reckon I can fix you up, all right," Allwood said in a pleased tone. "I don't carry much of a stock anymore. Most of the folks that lived here in Goose Creek have moved on."

"Some reason for that?"

"No, nothing special. Place just sort of died. The government surveyors come along and cut a new road about ten miles west of here, and people traveling stick to it. Same goes for the stage line," Allwood said, beginning to assemble the deputy's order. "Only one comes by here now, and that's only once a week. . . . You looking for a place to spend the night? I got a room at my house that I rent out. Can give you supper and breakfast, too. The wife's a real good cook."

Thomas gave that a thought. It was a tempting suggestion, but he'd already lost too much time on what virtually amounted to a snipe hunt. Best he head south as soon as possible and try to pick up the bank robber's trail—likely somewhere around where he and the sheriff's posse had cornered the other two outlaws.

"Obliged for the offer, but I figure I'd better head back. Missed the man I'm hunting somewhere along the way, and I've got to see if I can pick up his trail."

"Lot of country between here and Cheyenne," Allwood said, pushing the items Thomas had ordered together on the counter. "Man can head out in about any direction he wants and mighty soon lose himself—and anybody following him, for all that matter."

"Can't argue that. How much do I owe you?"

Allwood scratched some figures on a scrap of paper with a stub pencil. "Oh, three dollars'll cover it. Comes to a few coppers more'n that, but I always like to deal in even money. Maybe—" The storekeeper paused, studied Thomas. "Expect that sounds a mite high to you at that, but grain's a bit dear up here."

So is everything else, the deputy thought, digging into a side pocket for the necessary cash, but he said nothing; merchants manning a lonely, deserted outpost like Goose Creek were entitled to a little extra profit. Paying off, Newt collected his purchases, nodded a farewell to Allwood, and returned to his horse.

Storing the articles away in his grub sack and saddlebags, he mounted up and doubled back down the faintly visible tracks of the street.

"Well, you learn anything from John?" Morland called in a jeering voice as he passed.

Thomas shook his head. "Said he hadn't seen a stranger in weeks."

"Just what I told you! Beats all how some folks can't take a man's word for nothing. You riding out?"

"Back the way I came," the deputy answered. "Got a feeling I'll find that outlaw right about where I lost him."

"Yeh, maybe you will, Deputy. Good luck."

Thomas raised his hand and touched the brim of his hat with a forefinger. "So long—and same to you."

11

"Want you to know this, Dave," Nathan King said as they drew near the ranch, "I'm obliged to you for standing by me back there."

Gunnison shrugged. "You didn't think I'd back off, did you?"

King shook his head. "Way things have been going, a man hardly knows what to expect. Sometimes best friends turn out to be enemies."

"Signed on with you to work. Meant it."

"Appreciate that, but I wouldn't blame any man for pulling out under the circumstances. . . . Know you don't think I should've let them three high-binders off easy like I did, but hell, it ain't in me to shoot a man down in cold blood."

"Not something I'd like either," Dave said, "but sometimes there's a need."

"That mean you would've gone through with shooting them?"

Dave brushed at his mustache absently. "Can't answer that because I don't know for sure what I'd do until I come face to face with it. One thing for sure, their kind running around wild killing and lynching and burning down folks' homes sure don't deserve to live."

"You ever kill a man?"

"Nope. Got the notion a couple of times, but never did."

"Can understand that. I maybe talk now and then like I'd use my gun, but I've got my doubts I ever could—even against one of the outlaws that're running loose around here."

"Came down to using your iron to protect your wife or stop some of that bunch from burning down that fine house and barn of yours, I'll bet you'd not think twice about it. . . . Been wondering why the army hasn't stepped in and taken a hand to stop the trouble up here. There's a fort close by. Seems to me like this has gotten way too big for the law."

King half-turned in his saddle and looked back over the trail they were following. It was near dusk, and the range had a faint golden shine to it. They'd had a fairly wet winter, and the grass had come early.

"I reckon they'll be dealing themselves in pretty soon. Don't see nobody following us. Them three were the only ones around, seems."

That was hard to believe, Dave thought, considering the number of Regulators that had been seen in the area, but maybe he and King had been lucky. One thing was certain now, however: the rancher had declared himself when he shot, accidentally or otherwise, the man called Murph, and it was doubtful the Major, if the three were working for him, would let that pass. It was a well-known fact that absolute control depended upon absolute domination.

*   *   *

Bettina was standing at the back door when they rode in, a relieved smile on her lips. She followed them across the hardpack to the corral, where they drew up and dismounted.

"I was worried," she said, going to King. "You were gone so long. Was there trouble?"

"Some. I'll tell you about it later," the rancher replied, beginning to remove the saddle from the horse he was riding. "Anything happen around here?"

Bettina shook her head. In the fading sunlight her dark hair had taken on a faint reddish glint, and the color of her eyes appeared to be a deeper blue.

"No, nothing. Jubal left."

"Where's Hollander?"

"Said to tell you he was going back out and keep an eye on the herd."

King shook his head. "Dutch has been looking after the stock all day—was Jubal's turn to take the night watch."

Dave, hanging his saddle on the top rail of the corral, turned to the rancher. "I'll spell him. Have to get me another horse, though. Mine's about done in."

"Spare mounts in the corral back of the bunkhouse. Take your choice," King said, adding his gear to the top rail. Opening the gate, he turned his horse into the enclosure. "I'll ride out about midnight and relieve you so's you can get some sleep."

Dave took the bridle off his horse, turned the tired gelding into the corral with King's, and started toward the rear enclosure where a half-dozen or so other horses were standing. He was dead on his feet and could use some sleep, but he reckoned he could hold out till midnight.

"You know where the herd is?" King called after him.

Dave halted. "Not exactly sure, but I've got an idea."

"Cut west after you leave the yard, and keep going. We've got the stock grazing in a meadow about a mile from here. . . . I'll feed your horse."

Gunnison nodded and continued on. Selecting a wiry little bay that offered no objection when approached, he slipped the bridle on, led the animal back to the front corral, and strapped on the rest of his gear. The Kings were nowhere to be seen, and he assumed they had gone into the house. Mounting up, Dave rode out of the yard. Following the directions given him by the rancher, he shortly located the cattle and settled quietly in a grassy swale. He had scarcely gotten the herd in sight when Hollander challenged him from behind a stand of brush.

"Close enough! Any closer and I'll blow you out of that saddle."

"Easy, Dutch," Dave called. "It's me—Gunnison. I've come out to spell you."

There was a long few moments of silence and then Hollander's voice, coming from a bit nearer, said, "Sure, I recognize you now. Ride on in."

Dave continued on down the slight grade to where Hollander's horse was tethered to a young aspen.

"Head on back to the ranch, get yourself some shut-eye," Dave said, staying in the saddle. He wanted to ride around the herd, get an idea of how bunched it was before he settled in.

"Them's mighty welcome words," Hollander said in a heavy voice. "I'm so dang beat I couldn't hit the ground with my hat, but I misdoubt you're much better off if you've been riding all day."

"Nathan said he'd come out about midnight and take over so's I could go back and catch a few winks."

Dutch nodded. In the pale light he was a slim, bent shape with his face completely shaded by the wide brim of his hat.

"Expect you and me best work out some kind of a timetable," Dutch said as he climbed wearily onto his horse. "You and Nathan run into that bunch I was telling you about?"

"Sure did," Dave replied, and briefly recounted what had taken place.

When he finished, Hollander wagged his head slowly. "Expect the fat's in the fire now," he said, and rode off into the night.

There was little doubt of that in Dave's mind. The Regulators would strike back. But he guessed trouble was bound to come to Nathan King. The passing neighbor had brought word that King had been put on the Regulators' death list so the incident up near the buttes would have changed little, other than perhaps hurrying up retribution.

The herd was quiet in a fairly deep bowl and seemed to be bedded for the night. Dave, picking as his point a spot a hundred yards or so below where he had found Hollander, dismounted and, hunched shoulders to a large rock, stared off into the night.

Overhead, the sky was an arching shroud across

which a myriad of sparkling stars were scattered, and all about him was the breathless beauty of the Wyoming grassland, its soft silvery sheen darkened here and there by coulees overgrown with sage or shadowed by an occasional tree. Coyotes howled in the distance and back in the direction of King's ranch a dog was barking—one of the two or three he'd seen hanging around the place, Dave reckoned.

It was a beautiful, peaceful world, Dave thought ... but only on the surface. Beneath the calm veneer lay a seething volcano of violence that was certain to erupt only too soon, but he was glad he had elected to stay. Disregarding the fact that being a working hand on Nathan King's combined ranch and homestead undoubtedly would be good cover insofar as the law was concerned, the knowledge that he would be doing something worthwhile filled him with satisfaction.

Ever since he was old enough to strike out on his own, Dave Gunnison had lived a nomadic, uncaring life, thinking only of himself and of what would benefit him most. Up until the time of the ill-fated attempt to rob the Cheyenne bank, he'd not gotten on the wrong side of the law, although he had come dangerously close to it on occasion. Looking out for himself, doing the things that required the least stress and strain while providing him with the few necessities his way of living required, was all that ever really interested him.

He was at a loss as to why he should so abruptly have a change of attitude. Why was he willing to take on a job with Nathan King, a man he'd never met before that day, and put his life on the line in a range war that was of no interest to him?

It wasn't solely a means for avoiding the deputy, who had continued on north and probably was now somewhere in Montana or on his way to Canada searching for him; Dave had only to keep moving to avoid the lawman. He guessed it was like someone had said, "everything has its time." Where he was concerned, he supposed the day had simply come for him to do something of value with his life.

A sudden clicking of horns and scuffling of hooves brought Dave to his feet. Something had disturbed the cattle. Moving hurriedly to his horse, he mounted and rode quietly to the far end of the swale where the noise had seemingly come from. Drawing near, he slowed the bay and allowed the horse to proceed at a walk.

A few of the steers were moving about, but he could see no reason for their restlessness—at least no human cause. It could have been a coyote braver than usual, or a wolf venturing in close, or even some smaller animal that had roused them. Dave slouched in the saddle, waited out a good quarter-hour, and when there was no further commotion, he rode on, circling the herd as he did and halting once again by the rock he'd chosen as his post.

They would need to arrange a regular system for keeping watch over the cattle—just as Dutch Hollander had said—Dave thought when he'd settled down. He and Hollander could take turns at the day and night watches, which would allow Nathan King to attend to other ranch and farm chores while being more or less in reserve should trouble develop.

Fortunately King's herd was small, and since the range was in good condition, the cattle would require but little attention insofar as grazing and watering were concerned. The danger lay in the Regulators, or the outlaws, endeavoring to rush in, stampede and kill or rustle some of the stock.

He'd hash it over with King in the morning. If he was going to pitch in and help the rancher, he aimed to do it right. One thing he'd learned, and learned the hard way was—

The rattle of gunshots broke the night's stillness. Dave lunged to his feet and rushed to his horse. Outlaws or members of the Regulators were stampeding the herd. Jerking the reins free of the brush clump to which he'd tied them, Gunnison vaulted into the saddle and, gun out, spurred the bay toward the shots.

12

The cattle were already beginning to move. Dave, galloping toward the lower end of the swale where the rustlers or Regulators, whichever they were, had started shooting, saw the solid mass of dark hides and glistening horns surging up the hollow. Unfamiliar with King's range, he was uncertain what lay in that direction, but thought it was all open country. If so, the cattle would come to no great harm but would simply run themselves out and finally stop.

More shots sounded, sharp and definite above the sudden drumming of the now running stock. Dave caught a glimpse of two riders, and then a third. They were whipping back and forth along the rear of the frightened herd, urging the stock on with their shooting. Dave flung a hurried shot at the nearest of the riders. The bullet evidently passed close, for the man pulled up abruptly and, wheeling, joined his two companions. All three then opened up on Gunnison.

Dave cut right as bullets dug into the turf near him and whistled softly as they sped by. Swerving in behind a stand of brush, he reloaded as the bay thundered on with the three riders, firing as they came, still coming on.

Reaching the far end of the brush and weapon now ready, Dave veered once again—this time going left. In so doing, he put himself above the marauders and at a slight advantage. For a few brief moments he was lost to them, and making the most of his advantage, Gunnison waited until he had a clear view of the raiders. He leveled his weapon on the nearest man and pressed off a shot.

The rider yelled and swung away as the bullet drove into him. The two men with him came about and, locating Dave, began to fire. But Gunnison was already racing away. Reaching the boulder near which he had spent the earlier hours, Dave guided the heaving bay in behind it and halted. Steadying himself, he drew a bead on the rider coming straight for him and triggered a shot. In that same instant he caught sight of the remaining raiders—three of them—bearing down on him from the right.

Immediately Dave cut the bay hard left and fired point-blank at the man closing in on him from the side. The rider dropped back, but Dave was uncertain whether his bullet had found its mark or had simply come close, unnerving the man. Regardless, for the moment he was in the clear, and spurring the bay, he rushed on down grade through the pale light.

He could hear yelling somewhere behind him, audible above the fading rumble of the running herd. He had gained little on the raiders, and now, bent low, he pointed his horse toward the hedgelike stand of brush that stood on the west side of the swale. If he could make its dark shadows, he'd have a good chance of shaking the four riders now in pursuit and firing sporadically at him.

He couldn't tell where the bullets were striking. Somewhere behind him, he supposed. His lead and the fact the men were using their six-guns rather than rifles from the backs of running horses were a hindrance to any degree of accuracy.

He reached the brush, a combination of sage, laurel, and what looked like aspens, unhurt. It made no difference what the dense growth was; it offered good cover from the oncoming raiders— outlaws or Regulators. They had ceased firing and were now yelling to one another. One, apparently the leader, ordering the others to separate, circle the tall, hedgelike growth, and cut him off.

A hard grin pulled at Dave's mouth. He was in as tight a spot—other than the failed bank robbery—as he had ever been. Allowing the bay to slow to a walk, he took advantage of the moment to replace the spent cartridges in his .45, then he listened to the night. He picked up the sounds of horses—two of them, he thought— rushing across the east side of the brush, the riders apparently following the shouted order to cut him off. Logically, the remaining two riders would be coming around the south end of the hedge.

Gun cylinder filled, Dave checked the loops on his gun belt. Ony seven more rounds—and that meant he couldn't keep up a running fight with the raiders for much longer. But that was not the pressing problem; the marauders were circling to come at him from opposite sides. That left him with two choices; strike out across the open range and hope to outrun the riders, or head directly into the brush hedge and hope to make it through to its opposite side without the raiders hearing and realizing what he had done.

The latter course was the more sensible. Immediately he turned the gelding into the brush. After a few paces the bay balked, refusing to breast the tough springy growth. Dave came off the saddle at once and, stepping out in front of the horse, grasped the animal's headstall and began to force a path through the growth. The bay followed along willingly enough as Gunnison, picking his course through the tangle, cleared the way.

"You see anything of him?" The voice, harsh and angry, was alarmingly close.

Dave halted instantly, careful to make no sound while the raiders paused in an effort to locate him.

"He sure'n hell didn't come around this end," a heavily accented voice drawled.

"Didn't double back neither. Means he's still around here somewheres."

"He could've kept going—west," a third man suggested.

"Was watching for that, and he didn't. He's got by us somehow."

"Hell, why don't we forget it?" the drawling voice suggested. "We've done run off that squatter's herd, killed maybe a half a dozen of his steers. That ought to be enough to set him to thinking."

"No, that ain't enough. I've got a hunch he's the wise-acre jasper that was with that squatter when they jumped Gates and plugged Murph. Aim to teach them both that nobody shoots a Regulator and gets away with it."

"Well, I'm betting whoever this is we cornered got away from us somehow. I'm for heading back to the ranch."

"Go ahead then, dammit! I ain't quitting till I nail that bird."

A long silence fell after that, one broken only by a rustling among the dead leaves in the brush and the continuing howl of coyotes well in the distance.

"All right, Keech," the man with the drawl said finally. "We'll stay with you long enough to circle this damned brush once more, but if we don't spot him, we're pulling out."

"Fair enough," Keech replied. "One of you stay here just in case he shows up. The rest of us'll circle back to the hollow."

At once the faint thud of the Regulators' horses moving off reached Dave. He stood motionless in the weak star and moonlight filtering down upon him through the brush, and again considered what his best move would be. The three other raiders would soon reach the far side of the thicket, making it foolish to continue in that direction. That left him with no choice other than to deal with the soft-spoken man assigned to wait and watch for him.

Leaving the bay, Dave turned about and quietly picked his way back to the west fringe of the brush. Halting just within the thick growth, he glanced about for the raider. The man was surprisingly close—out of his saddle and hunkered on his heels no more than ten feet away. Grim, pistol in hand, Dave cut back and worked his way silently toward the hunched figure.

Reaching a point directly behind the man, Dave took a deep breath, gathered his muscles, and stepped quickly out of the hedge. The raider, alerted by a faint crackling of dry twigs, twisted about and started to rise. His mouth opened as he framed a yell. Dave's pistol crashing down on his skull silenced the cry of surprise before it found voice.

As the man fell heavily to one side, Dave pivoted and shouldered his way back into the brush to his horse. Taking up the gelding's reins, he led the animal into the open and, vaulting into the saddle, started for the upper end of the brush hedge. In that moment gunshots broke out in the swale.

A grin once more crossed Gunnison's lip. That would be King and Dutch Hollander. They evidently had heard the earlier shooting and had come to help. Wheeling about, Dave put spurs to the little bay and sent him racing for the lower end of the hollow. The raiders, attacked from the opposite point, would understandingly make a run in that direction.

He reached the last of the brush with the rattle of gunfire in his ears and the smell of powder smoke in his nostrils. As he rounded the last of the thicket, he caught sight of three riders streaking off across the range. Raising his gun, Dave began to throw shots at them, adding his fire to that of King and Hollander, racing across the swale after them.

The Regulator party was well beyond reach of the handguns, and Dave, curving in toward the rancher and Hollander, who also had stopped their shooting, settled back on the bay and reloaded his weapon as he approached the two men.

"You all right?" King called as they drew together.

"All right," Gunnison replied. "They stampeded the herd. You spot it anywhere when you come up?"

"Up the ways a piece," Hollander said. "At a water hole. They'll be there waiting."

"Heard one of them say they'd shot a few head."

"Counted six when we rode through the hollow after that bunch," King said wearily. "Could be more."

"They'll be laying together," Dave said. "I got in on it right at the start and kept them from following the herd. Think I winged one of them, but I ain't sure—and I've got one laying back there behind the brush."

"Dead?"

"No, just knocked cold. Couldn't shoot because it would have drawn the others. I'll go get—"

"Forget it," King said. "Like as not, he's gone if you didn't tie him up. Anyway, what would we do with him? I ain't for lynching and we'd probably never get him to Buffalo and the sheriff."

"About right," Hollander agreed, shaking his head. "Sure looks like we're in the mud now with both feet. Too bad we can't get word to that Cree village about them dead cows. Shame for all that meat to go to waste."

"For sure," the rancher said. "Let's get back to the ranch. No sense us setting here in the cold talking. Can round up the stock tomorrow. That bunch ain't likely to come back again tonight."

13

"Was thinking last night while I was out there night watching that we ought to come up with some sort of plan for looking after the herd and the rest of your property," Dave said. "Dutch has got the same idea."

They were at the table that next morning eating breakfast and discussing the raid that had occurred. None of them had gotten much sleep—three, maybe four hours at most—but the spread Bettina had set before them—fried eggs, bacon, buttered hot biscuits and honey, and strong black coffee—had generated new life in each of them.

"What've you got in mind?" King asked.

"Way it looks seems like it's going to be just the three of us," Dave replied, and glanced at Bettina, who was studying him intently, her dark blue eyes bright. "Not counting your missus, of course."

"I can do my share," Bettina said quickly.

"Yes'm, I figured that, but I'm talking about looking out for the cattle and the house."

"I can use a rifle."

Dave nodded. "Expect you can all right, but I

figure this needs to be worked out between Nathan, Dutch, and me."

"I can look out for the house," Bettina persisted, and then looked away as King silenced her by raising his hand.

"Let Dave talk, Bett. After what he done for us yesterday and last night, I figure he's a man who ought to be listened to."

Bettina smiled and nodded slightly to Gunnison. "Yes, we owe you a lot, Dave—and I'm especially grateful to you for standing by Nathan the way you did when you ran into those three renegades. If he'd been alone, I hate to think what might have happened."

"No thanks needed," Dave said. Apparently King had given her full details of the encounter with the Regulators. "Just glad I was able—"

"Let's get to this plan we're thinking about," Dutch cut in irritably, a forkful of eggs and bacon halfway to his mouth. "What've you got in mind?"

"Just this—you and me will split up riding her, one of us taking the night shift, the other the day. We can trade off every week."

"Where does that leave me?" the rancher asked, watching Hollander nod his approval.

"Leaves you free to sort of look after everything," Dave explained. "You can handle whatever needs being looked after right around here—sort of oversee it all."

Hollander continued to nod. "That'll let you be handy in case them Regulators hit us again. We could fire a signal—two quick shots. That'd mean Dave or me was needing help, and you and whichever one of us is off sleeping are to come in a hurry."

"It'll work both ways," the rancher said. "If any of that bunch shows up here and I can't handle them alone, I'll use the same signal."

"Right."

Bettina sighed wearily. "Oh, I wish this terrible thing would end! Seems we've had nothing but trouble since that blizzard—"

"Ain't no doubt of that," King said, leaning back in his chair, a cup of coffee in his stubby-fingered hand. "Nobody'll hire out to work, not even the Canucks or the Indians. We can just about forget a garden this year—no time to tend it myself."

"What'll we be doing about hay for next winter?" Dutch wanted to know.

"Have to buy it in town, I reckon. There'll be some growing in the south field, but not enough."

"Something else," Hollander said. "After talking to Jesse Haines, I figure we best be careful—all of us—about going into town. Sure oughtn't to none of us go in alone."

"The town run by the Regulators?" Dave asked.

"No, it ain't that. The town's against the Major and them Regulators—it's the miles in between here and it we've got to worry about. Never can tell when some of that bunch is laying in wait for folks like us on the way to town."

King nodded. "Glad you brought that up, Dutch. . . . Bett, you best figure on not leaving the place until things settle down."

"Have you any idea when that might be?" the woman asked, frowning.

"Probably be some time—leastwise it'll be until the army decides to step in and straighten things out."

"We're running low on supplies. I really ought to go into town and—"

"You make out a list of what we need. I'll take Dutch or Dave and drive in after it," King said, and swore softly. "Hell of a note when a man has to live with a gun in his hand. Country ain't near as civilized as folks like to think."

There was quiet around the table for several moments as Bettina refilled the coffee cups, and then Hollander, thrusting a hand into his pants pocket, produced a silver dollar.

"Reckon we ought to settle right now who's going to do what. I'm flipping this here coin for us, Dave. If it comes up head, you'll take the day shift for the next week, if it's tails, you ride night herd."

"Suits me," Gunnison said, and watched as the older man sent the coin spinning into the air. It fell to the floor next to Nathan King's chair. The rancher bent over and looked at the bit of shiny silver.

"Heads," he announced, picking up the coin and returning it to the old cowhand. "Guess you draw the night turn, Dutch."

Hollander shrugged, glanced at the silver dollar. "Won this down at the Hog Ranch. Been my lucky piece ever since—up to now. Sure hope this don't mean my luck's running out."

"I'd as soon take the night watch as the day," Dave said. "We can start swapping later on."

"Nope, you won the toss," Dutch said, and pushed back from the table. Rising, he started for the door, hesitated, and faced Bettina. "I won't be bothering you for dinner. I'll just get along with a big breakfast till suppertime."

"You going back to bed?" King asked.

"Got some fixing to do on my saddle first. All that hard riding last night sort of busted loose the lacings on one of the stirrups. . . . You aim to move the herd in closer?"

King nodded. "Figured Dave and me'd drive the cattle to that water hole east of here. We ain't grazed that section since last summer, and being a sort of valley, we won't have no trouble holding the stock there for long as we want."

"Be a right good place," Dutch agreed. "Besides, it's close," he added, and continued on for the back door.

Dave got to his feet. "Expect I'd best be earning my keep. That water hole and valley, just where—"

"I'll give you a hand," King said. "Probably take both of us to round up the herd and drive it to the place I was talking about. Go ahead and saddle up, I'll meet you at the corral."

Gunnison, making his thanks to Bettina for the fine meal, took his leave. Crossing the yard, he entered the fenced area where the horses were. He cut out his own bay for use and, leading the gelding out of the enclosure, saddled and bridled it. That done, he refilled his cartridge belt from the box of shells he carried; then he unhooked his canteen from the saddle horn, crossed to the pump at the horse trough, and pumped the container full. As he was screwing the cap down tight, the sound of footsteps off to the side brought him around. It was Bettina King.

She was wearing a white housedress with a

yellow apron across its front, and in the bright, warm sunshine, with a light wind ruffling her dark hair, she made a fetching picture. Forgetting the canteen for the moment, Dave stared at her in frank admiration.

"I brought you some lunch," she said, handing a cloth-wrapped package to him. "There's a couple of sandwiches and a piece of pie. Try not to mash it."

Dave nodded. "I'll carry it inside my shirt. Sure am obliged to you, Mrs. King."

"Bettina. You don't need to be formal with me. No one else around here is."

Somewhere in the field beyond the corral a bird was whistling cheerfully, filling the morning quiet with its happy song.

Bettina listened for a few moments and then brought her attention back to Dave. "I want to thank you again for what you did yesterday."

"My job to look after the cattle," Dave said.

"I don't mean that. I meant when you and Nathan ran into those Regulators—outlaws, I call them. Nathan's a good honest man, but he doesn't know how to deal with their kind."

Dave grinned. "You could be wrong there. He handled them just fine. I just backed him."

Bettina smiled. "Thank you for saying that. I've never known a better man."

"Only been around a short time, but I reckon I can say the same," Dave said, and then, prompted by a streak of impoliteness not usual to him, voiced the question that had crossed his mind several times. "This has been bothering me ever since we met, and I know it ain't none of my business, but how did it happen a real pretty woman like you, who probably had a lot of beaus, would marry a man maybe three times her age?"

Bettina drew up slowly. The bright smile faded from her lips, and anger filled her eyes.

"You're right—it's none of your business," she snapped, and pivoting on a heel, marched stiffly back to the house.

Embarrassment and shame flooded through Dave. What in the world possessed him to ask Bettina such a question? It not only was none of his affair, but it was prying no man should ever be guilty of. Angry at himself, Dave finished capping the full canteen and headed back across the hardpack for his horse.

14

As Dave was swinging up into the saddle, Nathan King came out of the house and across the yard to join him. Dave steeled himself for an encounter with the rancher. King had every right to call him down for the inexcusable question he had put to Bettina.

"You figure you know where the herd is?" King asked as he halted beside the bay.

"North of here somewhere—a bit west."

"Right. They'll be at a water hole that's over that way. You go ahead, start. The wife reminded me of some farming chores I've neglected and that I'd best take care of. When that's done, I'll ride out and join you. Just head the cattle in this direction—place where I aim to put them is just east of here. . . . Here, take these field glasses of mine. Can use them to keep an eye on the country."

Dave sighed inwardly as he accepted the glasses. Evidently Bettina had said nothing to Nathan about their conversation, or else the rancher was choosing to ignore it. Either way, it brought a flow of relief to Dave, but the guilty feeling of having asked so personal a question still lay heavy on his mind. Nodding to the rancher, he put the glasses in his saddlebag and, raking the bay with his spurs, rode off.

The hardpack behind him and out on the range, a faintly yellow carpet stirring gently in the light wind, he struck a course northwest. Well in the direction of the rugged Big Horn Mountains he could see three widely separate smoke plumes. More homesteaders or small rancher's homes going up in flames, thanks to the Regulators, who were taking advantage of the trouble gripping the Wyoming plains, he assumed.

He shook his head angrily as he rode on. It was high time the army stepped in and did something to stop all the killing and destruction. Isolated as they were, the farmers and small ranchers were powerless to stand off raids by parties of perhaps a dozen or so experienced gunmen and outlaws. But King, or maybe it was Jubal, had said politics played a big part in the problem and it was doubtful the army would soon take a hand. It was the big cattlemen's hope that under the pretense of ridding the range of rustlers they could rid themselves of homesteaders and small ranchers as well.

Dave rode on for a good hour before he spotted the herd, fairly well bunched in a grassy swale where a glint of silver marked the presence of water. Moving around behind the cattle, he unhooked the rope he'd found in the bunkhouse from his saddle, and moving in on the herd, he began to haze them toward the east. The stock was reluctant to move, but finally he was able to start them drifting slowly away from the water and good grazing. Watching closely, Dave soon located the steer that appeared to be the leader of the herd—one of the half-dozen longhorns among the shorthorn Durhams—and maneuvered him about until he was out in front.

After that, it was not too difficult to keep the cattle moving. The old brindle steer, accustomed to being in the forefront, pushed out ahead and began to plod steadily on, doing his rightful job of leading the way, leaving it up to Dave to keep the stragglers from falling too far behind.

Moving the stock nearer to the house was a smart idea. With only three of them to keep an eye on the herd as well as King's other holdings, it was necessary to concentrate on the job as much as possible. King needed more hired help, there was no doubt of that, but it had been said that such was impossible; with trouble sweeping the range like the ceaseless wind, few men would elect to line up with the small ranchers or the homesteaders.

Late in the morning, with King's ranch house and other buildings now well to the south and west, Dave saw what he reckoned was the valley Nathan King had spoken of. It was a shallow, somewhat small hollow in the prairieland, but it was green with grass and ringed with trees and brush that concealed it well.

The water hole, while apparently shallow, would be sufficient for the small herd. The cattle, certainly not suffering for water and grazing, nevertheless broke into a trot when the valley came into sight with the old brindle well out in front. Reaching the lowest part of the hollow, the herd began to slow and scatter, most moving into the water, where they halted to stand and drink.

Dave kept in his saddle for another half-hour to make certain the cattle were settled, and then he rode to the west side of the area and drew up at the edge of the trees. He wasn't particularly hungry; Bettina's breakfast had been more than enough to hold him, but he felt the need for a cup of coffee.

Dismounting, he secured the bay where he could graze, and gathering a few small rocks, he arranged them in horseshoe shape. Building a small fire, he took the lard tin he used for such, poured a quantity of water into it, and set it over the flames to heat. That done, Dave sat back to wait.

When the water came to a boil, he dumped a short handful of the supply of crushed coffee beans he'd taken from the can kept in the bunkhouse for use of the hired help, allowed the liquid to surge up, and then set the tin off to one side to simmer. When he felt the brew was sufficiently strong, he stirred down the creamy froth with a twig and, getting his cup from his saddlebag, poured himself a drink.

He had just settled back on his haunches to sip at the steaming coffee when he caught sight of a rider. He set his cup aside instantly and came to his feet, subconsciously shifting the holstered gun on his hip forward to a more readily accessible position. And then, moments later, he saw it was Nathan King.

Dave had expected the rancher earlier, but he reckoned King had dropped far behind with his farm and ranch duties and it had taken him longer to catch up than figured.

"See you found the place," the rancher said as he rode up and halted.

Dave nodded and took up his coffee. "Could say the cows did the finding. Soon as they got in sight, they made a run for it. . . . More coffee here."

King shook his head. "Thanks, but I'm in kind of a hurry. You spot anybody hanging around on your way here?"

"Nope, not a soul. Did see some smoke over to the west."

The rancher nodded. "Seen that, too. More burnings, I suspect. Main thing I come for is to tell you that me and Dutch are going into town after those supplies. We figured this would be a good time to get all set up so's we won't be having to go in again soon. Dutch ain't getting any sleep anyway."

Dave finished his coffee and set the empty cup on one of the rocks near the dwindling fire. "This'll be the right time to go, all right. You want me to stay here?"

"For a while—two or three hours. Can look for the herd to stay where it is unless they get stampeded again. Don't get up no sweat if you see a bunch of Indians later on. One of the Crees happened by. Told him about those steers the renegades shot last night and that he and his people were welcome to them. They'll be showing up with drags to haul the meat off."

Gunnison signified his understanding. Then, "When'll you be back?"

"Can look for us about dark—maybe a little after. I'm not expecting trouble, but we could run into it the way things are."

"For sure," Dave said. "Too bad you're needing supplies right now." He was thinking about
the two incidents with the Regulators and remembering what he'd overheard while hiding in
the thicket. "No chance of holding off awhile?"

"No, we've run clean out of some things and
getting low on others. I aim to stock up heavy
and get set before matters get worse. Don't fret
none about it. My wife's doing enough of that for
all of us."

Dave shrugged, looked off to where the herd
was grazing contentedly. "Can't say as I blame
her none. I'll do this, I'll stay here for a couple of
hours, then ride in to the ranch and stay close. If
you and Dutch ain't back by eight o'clock, I'll
figure you've run into trouble. Eight o'clock give
you enough time?"

"Plenty."

"It's clear then. If you're not back by eight, I'll
head for town. You just might be needing help."

King brushed at his mustache and smiled. "If
we ain't back by then, we probably will. You
won't have no trouble finding us—there's only
one road in to Buffalo."

Deputy Newton Thomas pulled his buckskin
to a halt at the edge of the settlement and considered it thoughtfully. This would be Buffalo—
Buffalo, Wyoming, he knew; there were no other
towns in that area.

Touching his horse lightly with his rowels, he
rode on. He was tired and in poor humor, for he
had been in the saddle facing a stiff wind that
periodically buffeted him with blasts of sand

since early that morning. A good meal, a hotel
room with a soft bed, was what he needed, he
supposed.

So far his search for the fourth outlaw who
had attempted to hold up the Cheyenne bank
had failed. There had been no sign of the man,
and the riders he had encountered going to and
coming from the Montana border had professed
to have seen no one on the trail—which was
hardly believable but understandable. People,
Newt Thomas had learned long ago, were usually reluctant to give any information to a lawman—probably in fear of reprisal.

But the outlaw he sought was in the area, the
deputy was certain of that. They—he, Sheriff
Dawson, and the posse—had just overlooked him
somehow. He probably had been hiding somewhere in the grove that morning when they had
flushed out and slain his two companions. Actually, he had thought it a better idea to hang
around the area, perhaps the town itself rather
than ride clear to Montana in hopes of stumbling
across the outlaw on the trail, but Sheriff Dawson had thought otherwise. Now he'd made the
ride up Powder River and back and had turned
up nothing. He'd follow his own hunches from
here on.

He had wondered if he'd been lied to by one or
more of the men he'd talked to on the trail, and
thereby thrown off the outlaw's track. There were
hard cases running loose all over that part of
Wyoming, riding the trails during the night as
well as day, but none had fit the description of
the bank robber or admitted having seen him.
Seemingly the outlaw had vanished completely

from the world, which really was not out of the ordinary; a man could lose himself quickly in the broad, wild reaches of Wyoming with very little effort if he so chose.

But Newt Thomas had a feeling that was not what had happened. The outlaw, on the run since Cheyenne, undoubtedly poorly equipped to survive the trail, would need supplies. He would have to stop somewhere—but so far the deputy hadn't found a homesteader or a rancher where he had halted.

Considering all that as he rode slowly down Buffalo's main street, teeming with people moving about or gathered in groups, Thomas had a strong hunch that the chase was about over, that he would find his man here in this town or turn up information that would lead to him. And that was all important to the young lawman. The job as Laramie county sheriff waiting for him back in Cheyenne when he brought the outlaw in, dead or alive, was the culmination of his long restrained ambition.

Bill's Livery Stable ... Gem Restaurant ... Foote's General Store ... Powder River Bank ... Bon Ton Saloon ... Butterfield's Gun & Saddle Shop ... Cattleman's Hotel ... several more saloons and business houses. It was quite a town, Newt thought as he idly noted the signs on the buildings as he entered the settlement.

Abruptly Thomas veered the weary buckskin to his left as the black-lettered sign above the doorway to one of the structures caught his eye— SHERIFF'S OFFICE. It was the first place he needed to visit, then he'd head back down the street to the livery barn, stable the buckskin, after which he'd see about a hotel room and getting himself the meal his guts were clamoring for.

Halting at the hitch rack, vaguely aware of the hum of conversations in the street and on the broad sidewalks near him, of the fine dust haze hanging in the air, he dismounted, tied the horse to the rack's crossbar, and shouldering his way across the walk, entered the lawman's quarters.

A lone man about his own age and also wearing a deputy's star was sitting at a cluttered desk. Newt glanced about the walls plastered with calendar pictures, wanted posters, and a large map of the state, and then centered his attention on the deputy.

"Name's Newt Thomas," he said, extending his hand. "Deputy sheriff from down Cheyenne way."

The man at the desk got his legs under him and got halfway to his feet. "I'm Bert Cullen," he said, shaking Newt's hand. "Pleased to meet you."

"The sheriff around?"

Cullen sank back into his chair. "Nope, sure ain't. Went over to talk to the colonel at Fort McKinney and ain't back yet. Something I can do for you?"

"Was looking for a message from Cheyenne."

Cullen shook his head. "Sure ain't seen none, and I never heard the sheriff say anything about one. You up here looking for that fellow that robbed the bank?"

Newt Thomas nodded. "I am."

"Well, I wasn't here when that posse and the sheriff leading them rode in. Was out hunting for a killer that had ambushed a homesteader below town. But I heard what it was all about. Bank robber. That sheriff—Dawson, I think it was—your boss?"

"Yes. I was with him and the posse up to where we flushed out two of the outlaws. I went on after the third one."

"Never did find him, I take it."

Thomas shook his head. "Never did. Saw a lot of riders, talked to a few, but nobody claimed to have seen him either."

"Country's full of strangers," Cullen said. "This damn range trouble's sure got everything in a mess. You staying around?"

"Figure to. Got a feeling the man I'm hunting's not far away."

"You went up the Powder River, somebody said."

"Clear to Montana and back—no sign of him. Sheriff Dawson left you a description of him, I reckon."

Cullen nodded. "Yeh, and your posse did a lot of looking around town, especially in the saloons. Didn't turn up nothing or anybody that'd seen him."

"Well, he's got to be somewhere," Thomas said with a shrug. "Aim to go get myself a bite to eat, then take a room at the hotel. If you or the sheriff wants me, that's where I'll be."

"Good enough," Cullen said. "If that message you're looking for comes in, I'll carry it over to you."

"I'll be mighty obliged," Thomas replied, and wheeling, returned to the street.

No doubt Sheriff Dawson and members of the

posse had made a thorough search of Buffalo for the missing outlaw, but that was days ago. It would be different now, Thomas thought as he swung back into the saddle; the outlaw could have hidden in the groves or brush outside of town until the lawmen left and then come in. He'd have his own look about; he'd never been one to take things for granted.

15

Pouring the last of the coffee into his cup, Dave watched Nathan King lope back in the direction of the ranch. When he was lost to sight beyond a roll in the land, Dave finished off the drink, knocked the grounds out of the lard tin, and restored it and the cup to his saddlebags. That done, he crossed to his horse and, mounting, rode off toward the herd.

Keeping a short distance from the cattle, Gunnison walked the bay slowly around the stock in a broad circle while scanning the surrounding grassy plain with eyes narrowed to cut down the sun's glare. Well to the north he could see a blur that could be several riders moving toward the west. Halting, Dave studied the dark blot for a long minute and then, suddenly remembering, took the field glasses King had lent him from his saddlebags and trained them on the distant bit of motion.

It was a party of riders—seven in all, he saw, and moving as if in a hurry. Swinging his view back to the east, he picked up a thin plume of smoke twisting up into the cloudless sky. As he watched the streamer thickened. It could mean only one thing: another homestead or ranch house going up in flames, victims of the Regulators, or outlaws masking as such.

Continuing to sweep the horizon with the glasses, Dave picked up several more riders off to the south. They held his attention until they faded from view. The seven men headed west were also gone from sight, he saw, bringing the glasses back to bear in that direction.

Lowering the old pair of army vision aids, he put them back into his saddlebags and continued to circle the herd. An uneasiness was building within him—not for King and Dutch Hollander, who would shortly be on their way to Buffalo, some eighteen or twenty miles distant, but for Bettina. She would be alone at the ranch, and with parties of Regulators and outlaws roaming the range, she could be in danger.

After making a complete circle of the herd and finding the cattle quiet, Dave rode to a rise a quarter-mile or so to the north of the hollow and halted at the edge of a stand of brush. Leaving the saddle, he took the field glasses and the lunch prepared for him by Bettina, and moved to the highest point of the rise. Settling down facing the southwest—the direction in which the ranch lay—he unwrapped the sandwiches—fresh bread, tender sliced beef spread with butter and newly ground horseradish—and began to eat.

He could not see the ranch house and other buildings from where he sat, but riders coming in from the north or west and headed toward them would enter his vision. If such occurred, he would mount up and hurry to be with Bettina, just as he would if he saw smoke rising in that general direction.

Finishing the sandwiches and topping them off with the pie and a drink from his canteen, Gunnison continued his double vigilance, keeping close watch on the area where the ranch lay and on the herd. The sun, unimpeded in the vaulting blue arch of the sky, was warm, and the wind blowing was not strong enough yet to be disagreeable.

In the nearby brush chunky gray moles scampered about among the dry leaves and twigs, and once a hawk, evidently accustomed to feeding on the small mouselike creatures, flew in to perch on a rock close by. The bird hesitated briefly, bright hard eyes on Dave, and then, launching itself from its perch, flew off. Far to the west a half-dozen buzzards soared lazily in a wide circle, bringing to Dave's mind the steers that the raiders had killed the night before. He'd seen no signs of the Cree Indians who were to come and claim them, and he wondered if the scattered carcasses were the object of the broad-winged scavenger's attention.

Where he now sat he was uncertain just where the herd had been when the raiders struck, but the area over which the vultures were circling seemed to be in the right direction. He hoped he was wrong about that, hoped that the Indians had come and salvaged the beef, and thus beat the buzzards to a feast.

More riders appeared on the horizon an hour

or so later, again to the north as well as the south. The two parties were not close, but they roused again a worry in Dave for Bettina. There was far too much activity on the range and finally, around four o'clock, he could stand it no longer. Mounting up, he circled the herd once more and then rode back to the ranch.

All looked to be quiet as he came into the yard and drew up at the corral. The lack of trouble signs filled him with relief, and coming down off his horse, he turned the animal into the corral and started toward the house. His hand darted for his gun as the door opened and fell away as Bettina appeared.

"Something wrong?" she asked, frowning anxiously.

Dave shook his head. "Lots of riders on the prowl. Figured I'd best drop by and see if you were all right."

Bettina smiled. She seemed no longer angry at him for the stupid, impolite question he had asked, and he was pleased to see that.

"Everything has been quiet around here," she said. "Come inside. I've got coffee on the stove."

Dave followed the young woman into the house, relieved not only that she was all right but that he was again in her good graces. He'd never again embarrass himself—or her—by such thoughtlessness. Sitting down at the table in the kitchen, he watched her move about as she procured cups from a wall cabinet, filled them from the granite pot on the back of the stove, placed one before him while retaining the other for herself. He wondered then if Nathan King realized what a fortunate man he was.

"Did you have any trouble moving the herd?" Bettina asked as she took the chair opposite him. "Nathan was sorry he didn't get through in time to help."

"No trouble," Dave replied. "Managed to sort out the old leader bull, work him to the front, and get him headed in the right direction. Was easy going after that.... Looks like Nathan's all set for trouble," he added, motioning to another table placed near the window overlooking the backyard. Three pistols, a shotgun, two rifles, and a quantity of ammunition for each had been laid out and ready for quick use.

"Nathan says they'll have to kill him before they can burn down our place," Bettina said, her soft lovely features abruptly grim. "I feel the same way."

"Maybe it won't come down to that," Dave said gently, and took a swallow of his coffee. "Sure never hurt none to be ready, however.... You got any chores you'd like for me to do? Aim to stick around here now the rest of the day."

Bettina shook her head and then frowned. "Will the cattle be all right?"

"With all the trouble we've got around here, I figured I had to make a choice of being close to you or staying with the herd. You won. Expect your husband would agree."

Bettina smiled again, exposing even white teeth, while a glint of merriment filled her eyes. Again Dave wondered why she had married a man so many years her senior, but he wasn't about to make the same mistake he had earlier.

"I guess that's a compliment—choosing me over all those cows," she said, rising. "Expect I'd best start supper, have it ready for Nathan and Dutch. Are you hungry? If you are, that pie's still warming in the oven."

"I can wait," Dave said, getting to his feet. "That lunch you fixed me sure hit the spot. I'll go outside and have a look around."

Bettina paused, studied him quietly. A lock of her dark hair had come loose and was now curling down upon her forehead.

"You seem to think we're going to have trouble for certain," she said, brushing the wandering lock aside. "There some reason why?"

"Nothing I can hang my hat on, but there's too many riders running loose on the range. Kept an eye on them long as I could, but lost them, so I'm not sure exactly where they were headed."

Bettina bit at her lower lip. "I wonder about Nathan and Dutch. If they—"

"They're probably all right. Those riders were miles from where they are," Dave said hastily, hoping to allay her fears.

"Nathan said if he wasn't back by eight o'clock that you would ride into town after him."

"That's the plan. Chances are it won't be needful. They'll be showing up about dark."

But darkness came and with it no sign of King and Hollander. Bettina served Dave an evening meal, pointing out there was no reason to delay his eating any longer. She ate also, after which Gunnison again went outside to take care of a few chores and watch for the two men while Bettina did what kitchen tasks were necessary. That done, she joined him.

Together they sat on the bench that Nathan had built near the back door, silent and disturbed as they rode out the dragging minutes, listening all the while to the grunting and squealing of the hogs fussing over the last scraps of their food, the muted clucking of the chickens, and restless shifting of the cow in her shed and the horses in their corral.

The golden glow in the western heavens faded completely, and a little at a time, the stars began to appear in the darkening sky. Time continued to drag and then abruptly Dave got to his feet.

"Must be eight—even after. I'm riding into town."

"I'm going with you," Bettina said promptly, also rising.

Dave shook his head doubtfully. "Ain't sure that's a good idea."

"Why not? I can ride and I can shoot—and it's my husband who may be in trouble."

Dave gave that a thought, but he was weighing in his mind the relative danger of leaving the woman behind to be alone or taking her with him. Which would be the safer? It would be better to have her close by, where he could watch over her, he decided.

"All right. I'll saddle you a horse while you get ready to ride. That your saddle I seen hanging in the barn?"

"Yes, and my horse will be in there, too," Bettina answered. "A little spotted mare."

Dave struck out across the hardpack at once for the barn, his disturbed thoughts now on King and Hollander. He had a deep, uneasy feeling that something was terribly wrong.

16

The road to Buffalo was not a well-defined course, being used only by those few ranchers and homesteaders in that particular area. For the first ten miles or so it traced its way directly across the grassy plain, after which it cut a path through a stand of trees and brush for a short while and then once again broke out into open country.

Dave, with Bettina King riding at his side, kept the horses to a good lope, careful not to tire the animals but designed to reach the settlement as soon as possible. The night was clear and somewhat cool with a star-filled sky overhead. It would have been a most pleasant ride under different circumstances.

As they pressed on, Dave couldn't help but steal an occasional look at Bettina King. She had put on a pair of her husband's pants altered to size, and with them she was wearing a white shirtwaist over which she had a wool jacket. A man's narrow-brimmed hat sat forward on her head, covering most of her dark hair, which she had gathered into a bun on the nape of her neck.

Rigid, she stared straight ahead, worry evident in the quiet contour of her face and the firm set of her lips. Dave couldn't see her eyes clearly, but he thought they were partly closed and probably filled with a deep concern for Nathan.

Once she felt his gaze upon her and, turning, smiled faintly. He nodded hastily, returned the smile, and looked ahead, a sort of dissatisfaction running through him. Maybe, if he hadn't gotten off on the wrong foot when he was younger, he could have found himself a wife like Bettina King; but no, he had been too damn busy knocking about the country having a good time and doing all he could to avoid responsibility of any kind. Now it was too late.

Even if he should meet another Bettina King, although he had serious doubt another like her could exist, he would have nothing to offer. He was an outlaw with the law on his trail now, and his chances for ever settling down and leading a normal life were practically nonexistent.

"Town's not far—only a couple more miles," he heard Bettina say.

He nodded. "Figured we ought to be getting close."

"What had we best do first when we get there?" she said, grasping the stock of the rifle hanging in the boot from her saddle. Withdrawing the weapon a few inches, she let it slide back into place as if making certain it was free.

"Go to the store where you trade, see if Nathan's been there."

"That will be Lockhart's. We've been dealing with him ever since we've been in Wyoming. After that?"

"If Lockhart says Nathan and Dutch have been there, then we'll have to ask around, find out if they've left—and when."

"What about going to the sheriff?"

Dave was hoping to avoid talking to any lawman, but for Bettina's sake, he reckoned he could.

"There's the town now," the woman said. "I can see the lights of the houses and stores through the trees."

Minutes later they reached the edge of the settlement and slanted their horses toward a building off to the left that Bettina said was Lockhart's. A large number of persons were abroad, gathered in small and large groups in front of the business houses or milling about in the street.

"It's because of this trouble we're having with those Regulators," Bettina said, an edge to her voice when Dave remarked on the unusually large number of people out at that hour. "Everybody's up in arms over them.

"Hard to see why the sheriff can't do something about it."

"I guess he tried at first, but there's just too much against him. The big cattle companies are running everything. With all the money they've got, they can do what they please. I guess you might say they're the real law in Johnson County."

"Sure a bad way for things to be," Dave said as they made their way through the crowd to the general store's hitch rack.

"I guess the sheriff's a good man and means well, but some of our neighbors found out it was useless to go to him for any help. What we need is for the army to move in and hunt down these outlaws who call themselves Regulators . . ."

"And the outlaws who call themselves Regulators . . ."

"Yes—all of them. It's the only way there'll ever be peace."

They reached the rack and halted. Swinging down from their saddles, they tied their horses to the crossbar, climbed the two steps to the landing fronting the store, crossed, and entered. The place was well-lit by a half-dozen wall lamps. Lockhart, a tall spare man wearing a denim apron over his business clothing, came forward hurriedly to meet them, a frown on his thin face.

"Missus King! I sure didn't expect to see you," he said, and glanced questioningly at Dave.

"This is one of the men who works for us, Dave Gunnison," Bettina said, and as the two shook hands, added, "Has my husband been here?"

"Why, yes—him and Dutch Hollander. Been three or four hours ago. I filled the list he had, then he went on."

"You see them leave town?" Dave asked.

"Sure did. Fact is, him and Dutch and me went over to the Bon Ton for a drink. Nathan wanted to hear the latest about the range trouble. . . . It's all over now. Army come in finally. Ain't heard all the details yet, but they say it's all over."

"Oh, thank heaven," Bettina murmured, but her face was filled with worry. "I wonder . . . I wonder where Nathan is. Dave, could we have passed him on the road, do you think?"

"Only if they'd pulled off."

"That must've been what happened," Lockhart said. "They could've heard you coming, and way things've been, it's smart not to take any chances. Could've thought you were some of them Regulators, or outlaws, and got out of sight."

"Maybe," Bettina said, strain showing in her voice. "But I can't help worrying."

"Well, don't get too upset till you know for sure," Lockhart said as they moved toward the door. "I know Nathan. He can take care of himself. Dutch, too. . . . Wish I could've been of more help."

Dave nodded to the merchant and held the screened door open for Bettina. They crossed the landing, returned to their horses, and climbed back into their saddles. Dave threw a glance down the street. Several men were in front of the sheriff's office, one of whom looked familiar. Recognition came instantly. Dave quickly swung his horse about, placing his back to the man. It was Deputy Newton Thomas.

He had no difficulty in spotting the lawman; the fringed coat was easily identifiable as well as the rattlesnake band on his hat. Dave wasn't certain if the deputy had seen him or not, for there were several dozen persons milling about in between the sheriff's office and Lockhart's store. But Dave took no chance, and hat pulled low over his face, riding close beside Bettina King, he headed out of town.

Once they reached the trees, he glanced back. No one was following. He breathed easier. Apparently Newt Thomas, if he had even noticed him, had failed to recognize him—which was understandable. The lawman had only the description of the bank employee to go on, and it would have been very poor and sketchy at best.

"Do you think Nathan could have done what Mr. Lockhart suggested."

"Sure a good bet," Dave replied, but there was no real conviction in his mind. King would have been watching, too, and recognized them. "I aim to keep an eye on the road from here on, look for wagon tracks," he added, and halting, dismounted. Handing the bay's reins to Bettina, his eyes down, he began to walk ahead.

A short time later, as they were entering the area where brush and trees cut a wide band across the road, he found what he was looking for: the flat, clean imprint of a wagon wheel's iron tire. It was on the right-hand side of the road, which would indicate the vehicle was moving north.

Dave came to a halt. The impression had cut away from the road. The wagon was being driven off into the tangle of brush and large trees. A frown knotted Gunnison's forehead; this could be where King had pulled off if and when he heard Bettina and him coming, Dave thought as he looked off into the starlight-dappled grove, or it could mean the worst had happened—assuming the tracks were those of the rancher's wagon.

Again he studied the prints, looking now for those of the horses—and for ones made by riders. In the pale light it was difficult to locate any at first, but then he found where a horse had walked alongside the wagon. Suddenly grim, Dave turned, took the bay's reins from Bettina, and climbed back into the saddle.

"Maybe you best wait here while I scout on ahead, see where that wagon went."

Bettina made no reply, simply stared woodenly at him. Gun in hand, he rode deeper into the maze of trees and lesser growth now following a trail of crushed brush and torn branches left by the passing vehicle. Abruptly he came to a stop. He could see the vague, indefinite shape of two horses standing to the left of a large tree. A moment later Dave made out the wagon. Gun up and ready, he moved on, drawing nearer. A curse ripped from his lips and a tightness gripped his throat. There had been a lynching. Two men, heads twisted grotesquely to one side, were hanging from a limb of the tree. A sign of some sort dangled from the booted foot of each.

Off his horse, a sickness filling him, Dave moved closer, hoping against hope that the two would not be Nathan King and Dutch Hollander, but knowing in his heart that it would be. A few steps more and there no longer was doubt. The army had taken a hand too late for Nathan King and Dutch Hollander.

The signs, stirring slightly in the light wind, bore the scrawled inscription: RUSTLER.

Glancing over his shoulder to be certain Bettina had not followed, Dave hurried to the wagon. Climbing into the seat, he backed the vehicle to where the bed was beneath the two hanging bodies. Likely they had been standing in it while the ropes were put about their necks, after which it was driven out from under them.

Taking his knife, Dave slashed the rope from which Nathan King hung, and arms about the man's waist, he lowered the corpse into the bed of the vehicle. He turned then to do the same for Hollander, paused as movement nearby claimed his attention. His hand went automatically to the gun on his hip with the thought that the Regulators had returned. Tension left him in that next moment when he saw that it was Bettina. Apparently worried at his absence, she had followed him into the trees.

Returning to his grisly task, Dave cut down Dutch Hollander, aware that Bettina, off her horse, had rushed forward. Sobs tearing from her throat, she had climbed up into the wagon and was throwing herself upon the lifeless body. Quietly laying Hollander's body nearby, Dave listened to the wrenching sounds of her weeping for a long time, and then reaching down, he took her by the shoulders and gently pulled her to her feet.

"Best we get out of here," he said. "Bunch that did this could come back."

Bettina, holding a handkerchief to her lips to stifle her weeping, nodded and allowed Gunnison to help her to the ground.

"Why—why did this have to happen to Nathan?" she asked between sobs. "He was a good man, a kind one. He never hurt anybody."

"Usually the way it happens," Dave said, taking the woman in his arms in an effort to comfort her. "Reckon nobody's ever been able to figure out why his kind are always the kind to cash in first."

For a long minute Bettina stood close to Dave and then, once again in control of her emotions, turned away and started for her horse. "Like you said—we'd better go," she said, and then hesitated as Dave caught at her arm.

"Hate to ask this, but do you mind driving the wagon? I expect it's best for me to ride along behind, see that we're not being followed." He had pushed aside the purchases King had made at Lockhart's, and had taken the tarp that had covered them and drawn it over the bodies. "Aim to ride on ahead, too, sort of keep circling. Sure don't want any surprises."

Bettina said nothing, simply moved to the wagon, placed a foot on the hub of the left front wheel, and before Dave could assist, climbed up onto the seat.

"I'll tie your mare on behind," Dave said, leading the spotted horse up to the rear of the vehicle. "I—I want to say I'm mighty sorry this happened. Nathan was a fine man."

Bettina nodded. "I'll miss him," she said.

Dave finished tying on the mare, slapped the lines against the broad backs of the team, swung the wagon around, and headed off through the trees and brush for the road.

Dave crossed to the bay and climbed into the saddle. Anger was simmering within him—anger mixed with disgust and revulsion. The Regulators—it had to be them—had struck back, and no doubt they would do so again, this time at the ranch itself . . . and Bettina.

Newt Thomas, talking with Deputy Cullen and

several other citizens of Buffalo who had gathered in front of the sheriff's office, put his attention on the man and woman coming out of a general store across the street a short distance. From habit he mentally inventoried the man's appearance: mid-twenties, red shirt, colorless, faded pants, tan hat.

The rider did seem to fit the description of the outlaw he was trailing, and one of the horses standing at the hitch rack was a bay, but that could mean little; bay-colored horses were a dime a dozen.

And the woman—that didn't fit. The bank robber was a stranger insofar as they all knew, and this couple appeared to be well-acquainted— perhaps even married. Thomas turned to Deputy Cullen and pointed to the pair, now riding off.

"Know them?"

Cullen squinted in the direction of the departing riders and shook his head. "Sure don't. Woman maybe's a mite familiar, couldn't tell much about the man. Probably a couple of them homesteaders living west of here."

Thomas nodded absently. They didn't look like homesteaders to him; for one thing, the horses were riding stock and not heavy-bodied farm animals.

"Who runs that store?" he asked then, pointing to the establishment.

"Lockhart—Harry Lockhart," Cullen said, raising his voice to be heard above the nearby din and confusion. "One of the old-timers around here."

Newt Thomas nodded. "Think I'll go have a

talk with him. Maybe he can tell me who they were—leastwise the man. The woman don't matter."

"Expect he can," Cullen said as the Cheyenne deputy walked off.

17

When they were within a quarter-mile of the ranch, Dave swung in nearer to the wagon and, raising his hand, signaled for Bettina to pull up.

"I'm going on ahead, take a look around. Wait here."

He cut away at once, not waiting for any reply. Keeping to the shoulder of the road, taking advantage of the shadows, he made his way to the ranch. The lower corral was first in line after he passed the fields and garden, and walking the bay quietly along the side of the rail-enclosed yard, he reached the edge of the hardpack and halted.

Immediately one of the dogs sleeping near the bunkhouse roused and rushed forward barking furiously. At a command from Dave the animal quieted, and evidently recognizing Gunnison, it returned to the pile of gunnysacks that served as his bed. All appeared to be in order. The house, barn, and other structures stood silent in the moonlight, and the mere presence of the dog would indicate there were no intruders on the place.

138

But Dave, taking no chances, rode deeper into the yard, made a complete circuit of the ranch house, and finally convinced there was no danger, headed the bay back to where Bettina was waiting. Even in the pale light he could see the anxiety in her features.

"Everything's all right—fine," he said at once, relieving her fears. "Nobody's been around."

They continued on, Dave taking a last look at their back trail to assure himself they had not been followed by any of the Regulators—or Deputy Sheriff Newt Thomas—and finding no signs of either, he resumed his place ahead of the wagon.

He guessed Newt Thomas had not recognized him. There had been considerable distance filled with a dust haze between them; he and Bettina had not been under strong lamplight, as had the deputy. Those factors—abetted by the knowledge that the lawman had never actually seen him but had only a description to go by—eased Dave's mind considerably where Thomas was concerned.

The Regulators were something else. They had lynched Nathan King not only because he was one of the small rancher-homesteaders whom they declared were nuisances cluttering up the range but out-and-out rustlers as well; also as retaliation for King's treatment of the three Regulators he'd found on his land.

All of which added up to further reprisal, and this time Bettina and the ranch itself would bear the brunt of their callousness. Dave swore deeply. He was now in this so-called Johnson County War up to his eyeballs whether he liked it or not!

Reaching the front corral, Dave halted and, leaving the saddle, hurried to open the barn door so that Bettina could enter with the team and wagon. When he had the wide, hinged panel pushed back, she immediately headed the rig into the dark interior of the broad structure, filled with the odors of hay, leather, and horse droppings. Pulling to a stop, she allowed Gunnison to help her down.

Weeping was behind her now, although her features were drawn and wetness still shone on her cheeks as she turned to Dave.

"Nathan was a practical man. We had a drifter come by here a few years back—a carpenter by trade, actually. Nathan had him build two coffins." Bettina paused to get a firmer grip on herself. "They're in the storeroom in the back. Use them for Nathan and Dutch."

Dave nodded. "There anything else I can do?" he asked, lighting one of the lanterns hanging on the wall.

Bettina shook her head, started to move off, and then hesitated. "I'd like it if you'd put the coffins in here—in that first stall. Later on, I want to come down and sit with Nathan for a time. We can bury him and Dutch in the morning."

"I'll take care of it," Dave said, marveling at the young woman's strength. "You want me to tote the supplies Nathan bought up to the house tonight?"

"When you get time," Bettina said, and moved on to the wide doorway. Again she paused. Facing Dave, she said, "I see you left your horse out. Does that mean you'll be riding out tonight?"

Dave pushed back his hat in a gesture of exasperation. "You think I'd go off, leave you here like this?" he demanded. "Aimed to have a look at the herd after I got other things out of the way. Where'd you get the idea I might ride on?"

"Nathan. He said you were a drifter, that you didn't aim to stick around for long—especially if things got real bad."

Dave shrugged. "Don't recollect giving him that idea, but maybe I did."

"Then you don't plan to leave?"

"Nope, leastways not for a while. I'm sure not about to go riding out and leave you in the fix you're in."

"But Nathan said the law was after you. What if they show up here?"

Again Dave Gunnison's shoulders stirred. "Can't answer that. Reckon we'll just have to cross that creek when we come to it."

But that could be soon, Dave thought. Deputy Newt Thomas was in Buffalo, and no doubt he was busy asking questions. If he talked with Lockhart at the general store, chances were good the lawman's suspicion would rise and he could be expected to put in his appearance at the King place.

Bettina's features, soft-edged in the mellow light of the lantern, reflected her relief. "Thank you for staying, Dave. I don't know what I'd do if you left. . . . When you're through out here, come into the house. I'll make coffee and fix us a bite to eat."

Dave nodded. "Sounds real good," he said as Bettina continued on toward the house.

He watched her until she had opened the door, entered, and lamplight showed in the kitchen window. Then, carrying the lantern, he went farther into the barn in search of the storeroom. He located it in the southeast corner of the building, and pushing aside a pile of old harness, some burlap sacks, and a weather-thinned tarp, he freed the two board caskets and carried them up beside the wagon.

Noticing a pair of sawhorses, he placed them a proper distance apart in the barn's forward stall and set one of the elongated boxes upon them. A nail keg and a backless chair provided support for the other coffin. When they were in place, he laid the body of Nathan King in one, that of Dutch Hollander in the other after first emptying their pockets. It came to him then that neither man had any money on his person. Even Hollander's lucky dollar was missing. The two men had been robbed as well as murdered. Could that mean outlaws were guilty of the crime rather than the Regulators? Mulling that probability over, he nailed the lid on Hollander's coffin, but remembering Bettina's words, he left King's box open.

That disagreeable task done, Dave drove the wagon deeper into the barn, unhitched the horses, and taking the reins of Bettina's mare, led the animals to the corral. Removing their harness and gear and hanging it all on the top rail of the enclosure, he returned to the wagon and removed the supplies King had purchased from Lockhart and carried them to the house.

Bettina heard him coming and had the door

open when he arrived. Smiling his thanks, he set the boxes down and pivoted to go.

"Aren't you finished yet?" the woman asked. "I've got things all ready."

"Got to close the barn door," Dave replied. "Only take a minute."

Stepping out into the brightness of the night, Dave returned to the barn, lit another lantern, and hung it in the front stall. Locating another chair, he placed it near King's coffin, and then, taking up the other items he had removed from the rancher's pockets, closed the door and backtracked to the house.

Again Bettina was awaiting him. Halting before her, he turned over the articles he'd found on Nathan.

"Figured you'd want these," he said.

Wordlessly Bettina accepted them—a jackknife, a lucky piece, a bit of rawhide string, and a spent rifle cartridge. She studied them for a long minute and then laid the items on a nearby shelf.

"Was Nathan carrying any money?" Dave asked.

Bettina nodded. "Some. I don't know how much. He always paid cash when he bought anything." Frowning, she looked again at the items Gunnison had taken from her husband's body. "There's no money here—he was robbed, too!"

"That's the way it looks—and I ain't so sure now it was Regulators that did it."

Bettina was quiet for a few moments, and then her shoulders lifted and fell resignedly. "Does it matter? There's a pan of water on the bench out back if you want to wash up. I've put a clean towel there, too."

Dave suppressed a grin. With matters as critical as they were—her husband murdered, a longtime friend and employee also dead, and the very real possibility of a raid by the men who had done the killing hanging over her—she still could think of the small, inconsequential things.

Stepping outside to the bench, Dave washed up in the light coming through the kitchen window and then returned to where Bettina was sitting at the table. She had fixed them each a sandwich, heated up the pie he'd had a sample of earlier that day, and made coffee. They ate in preoccupied silence, with Dave leaving his chair several times during the light meal to step to the doorway and listen into the night.

All was quiet each time, and the hope they would be left alone at least until daylight grew stronger within him. But that was only the beginning. He couldn't see how Bettina King could remain on the ranch for any length of time, even with him around.

"You done any thinking, made any plans yet?" he asked, settling back to enjoy a second cup of coffee. "I mean, with Nathan gone, how can you figure to stay here alone? Even with hired help you—"

"This is my home. It always will be."

"But with those outlaws running wild burning down places, killing off stock and people, I don't see how you—"

"I'll hire on more hands, and with you around to boss them, everything will work out."

"The way Nathan talked there's nobody that'll hire out, especially to a small outfit."

"Somebody'll come along," Bettina said confidently. "You did. Besides, the army's stepped into the trouble here now and things'll change."

"Which will take time, so you can't figure on them right away—and just because you're a beautiful woman is no sign outlaws and the stray Regulators who ain't giving up because of the army will leave you alone. They've already lynched one woman—according to Jubal."

"I know," Bettina murmured, "but I'll stay. And I hope you will, Dave, for as long as you can. And thank you for the compliment. It's wrong to feel good about hearing something like that at a time like this, but it was still nice to hear."

Dave smiled faintly. "I don't see any reason not to mention it. Folks left behind have to keep on living despite whatever's happened to somebody that meant a lot to them."

Bettina was quiet for a long breath as she studied the last of the coffee in her cup. "I guess maybe I was pretty once—when I first married Nathan."

"No way for me to know what you looked like then, but I doubt you've changed much. You couldn't have."

Bettina produced a smile. "I can't answer that, but I can that other question you asked me earlier."

Dave frowned. "Question? Don't recollect what—"

"The one about why I married a man so much older than I am."

"Let it go. I had no right to ask. Plumb forgot my manners, else I wouldn't have, and it's been chawing at me ever since. You saying it's none of my business still goes, far as I'm concerned."

"I guess your asking me surprised me more than anything else," Bettina said with a half-smile. "Nobody else ever had, although I'm sure they'd thought about it. My answer to you was just sort of quick—angry, but I think I want you to know."

18

Dave rose and strode to the door. Pausing there, shoulder against the frame, he once more listened into the silver-filled halo of the night. A noise of some kind had drawn his attention, but it didn't come again, and turning on a heel, he resumed his chair.

"Want you to know you don't have to talk if it's painful."

"I'm all right," Bettina assured him. "I think I'll feel better for talking. . . . I met Nathan back in Kansas, near a town called Piedmont. My folks had a farm a few miles out of the town. Nathan—he had lost his wife to lung fever before he came to Kansas—had the place next to ours.

"He and Papa became close friends, helping each other, working together, and going hunting and fishing together—things like that. Nathan got to be like one of the family, I was only ten or twelve then, I don't remember exactly, but I can remember the two of them being like brothers.

"Everything went along fine, although farming the dry Kansas land and an occasional Indians scare made things hard. We didn't make much,

barely enough to stay alive, but we didn't mind—
at least I didn't. I guess it was because I didn't
know any better and was too young to feel the
pinch of hard times. And there was always Nathan around to help out if things got really bad.

"He'd lend Papa money, or bring over some
meat from a hog or calf he'd butchered, or maybe
it would be a sack of wheat or corn he'd ground
into flour. He was a lifesaver many times when
our fields didn't produce like they should—the
borers would get into the corn or maybe the fruit
trees, or there'd be a blight or maybe a plague of
grasshoppers. And on top of that, I'm afraid Papa
wasn't a very good farmer, but he tried hard. I
guess that's why Nathan liked him so much.

"And Mama liked Nathan very much, too. In
fact, I think she really adored him, although I
don't remember her ever letting him or Papa
know it. But I could tell, and I think Nathan
could, too. But he never took advantage of it, just
did all he could to help and make things easier
for her. She—"

Dave raised a hand for silence and, rising, again
crossed to the doorway to listen. Something was
disturbing the horses—there was no doubt of it.
Touching the butt of his .45 to make certain of
its presence, he stepped out onto the porch and
then down onto the hardpack. Walking swiftly,
he crossed to the corral.

Immediately he drew to a halt as a rank odor
assailed his nostrils. A skunk—probably hunting
about in the spilled grain in the corral for mice—
was the reason for the horses' nervousness. Stepping up to the rail fence, Dave glanced about
until he located the small animal, and picking up

a clod of dirt, he threw it at the obnoxious little varmint. The skunk halted its rooting about and then, when Gunnison hurled a second clod, ambled over to the fence and disappeared between the two lowest rails. Satisfied there was nothing more serious around—a cougar or a bear—Dave returned to the house.

Bettina had poured him a fresh cup of coffee and set another piece of warmed-over pie before him. He grinned as he sat down, and thanked her.

"I keep eating like this, I'll have to get a bigger horse to ride."

Bettina smiled. "Thin as you are it'll take a lot more than a few pieces of my pie. . . . What was bothering the horses?"

"Just a polecat hunting mice."

Bettina nodded. Then, "As I was saying, we all got along real well, like one family, helping each other and so on. Mama mended Nathan's clothes, made him a shirt now and then, and did things like that to repay him for all the nice things he did for us. She enjoyed doing it—the sewing, I mean—and Papa and Nathan and I always had nice things to wear even if there wasn't any place to go except church—and to school where I was concerned.

"I can still remember Mama sitting in her rocking chair—one that Nathan brought her—lamp on the table beside her, stitching something for one of us. She was beautiful, I always thought, and Nathan thought so, too, but he was honest about it.

"He told Papa more than once that he had a beautiful wife and that he should always cherish and appreciate her. And Papa would agree, and I know he did his best to do just that, but he had to work so hard to keep the farm going that it didn't leave him time for hardly anything.

"Then one night there was a fire. Papa had gone to bed. I had, too. Mama was in her chair sewing. Somehow the lamp got knocked over and the coal oil spilled on her and spread all over the floor. The room was a mass of flames before we knew what had happened. Papa and I tried to beat out the fire, but it had too much of a start, so he sent me over to get Nathan."

Bettina paused, lowered her head. "Even to this day I can hear Mama screaming. I guess I'll never get it out of my mind."

"I've heard folks say time takes care of everything," Dave said. "Maybe it'll fix that for you, too."

"Maybe. Nathan was asleep when I reached his house. He got up at once, pulled on some clothes, and we hurried back. When we got there, the whole house was ablaze. There was no sign of Papa. He had apparently stayed inside trying to help Mama, and they both burned to death."

"Mighty bad thing to happen," Gunnison said. "I can say I'm sorry, but I know it won't help much."

"Seems a long time ago—and the hurt's about all healed over. I was about fourteen when it happened, and since I had no relatives and no-where to go, Nathan took me in. We worked both farms together by hiring a man now and then to help, but pretty soon the story got around about Nathan living with a fourteen-year-old girl.

"To put a stop to that, we married, only it didn't end the wagging tongues. There was always talk about him and me, and people we thought were friends turned out to be the worst kind of gossips. Nathan finally got his fill of it, and one day when a man came by and offered to buy both places—Nathan's and mine—we sold out and moved up here to Wyoming. He had always wanted to raise cattle along with having a farm—he loved the soil—and he figured Wyoming would be a fine place to start over.

"Fortunately the man who bought our farms paid us in cash so we had plenty of money. Nathan, by hiring men from Buffalo, got this house and the other buildings put up right away, along with the corrals and such. Then he bought some stock, and later, when a couple of men from Canada—Canucks everybody called them—came by looking for work, he hired them to help him plow and plant the fields and put in a garden where I could raise vegetables. Everything started off real fine, and then that second winter a terrible blizzard hit."

Bettina's voice trailed off as she glanced toward the open doorway. The wind had risen and a pan or a bucket was clanking noisily on the porch.

"Was a bad one, I know," Dave said. "Jubal told me about it."

"We lost most of our livestock—cattle, some of the horses, pigs, the few sheep Nathan had bought and was hoping to start a flock with. It broke my heart to see the suffering in Nathan's eyes. He'd worked so hard to build up our ranch, and then to have it all but wiped out completely by that storm—it was hard to bear.

"But when it had all blown over, he started to rebuild everything—everything, that is, but the flock of sheep. He talked about buying a few this year, trying it again, but when all the trouble started, he gave up the idea."

Bettina hesitated, listened briefly to the banging of the pan. Then, "Now it's all over for him—all the things he wanted and hoped to do mean nothing."

She turned her glance to Dave. There were tears in her eyes. "You see now why I could never leave this place. My life is wrapped up in it, just as was Nathan's."

Rising, Bettina took a knitted shawl from a hook on the wall and draped it about her shoulders. "I'm going down and sit with him for a while," she said, moving toward the doorway.

Dave nodded. "I left a lantern burning."

"Thank you. Go on to bed if you like. You've had a long day, I know. I'll be all right."

Gunnison shook his head. "Not sleepy. I'll sort of hang around till you're back, then I aim to take a look at the herd."

Bettina smiled and continued on. Dave, coming to his feet, followed her to the door and halted there, watching until she had reached the barn and entered. Coming about then, he returned to the table, sat down, and with no particular relish, finished off his pie and coffee while he mulled over the question that had troubled men for ages: why did life have to end so early for good men—ones like Nathan King—while criminals, murderers, and the like continued to live, even prosper? It was and always had been beyond his understanding.

For an hour or so he sat in the chair thinking about that and other things, and then, as Bettina's footsteps sounded on the porch, he rose to meet her.

She halted, faced him. "I'd like to go with you to see the herd," and then added, "if you don't mind."

Dave said, "Jake with me." He could understand her reluctance to be alone. "I'll saddle your horse."

"No need. I'll ride double with you."

Gunnison made no comment, and taking up one of the rifles lying on the table near the window, he led the way to the corral, where the bay was waiting. Assisting the woman into the saddle, he handed the rifle to her and then swung up behind the cantle. It had been a long time since he'd ridden in such fashion, but the presence of Bettina, the smell of her hair, and the warmness of her back and shoulders against him made up for any discomfort.

Dave felt a twinge of guilt when he realized how he felt. Bettina King had just suffered a terrible loss and it was wrong to be thinking of her in such manner. But the pleasant thoughts were undeniable, and he could see no harm as long as he kept them to himself.

They found the herd resting quietly in the hidden valley, and after making a quiet circle around it, they started back for the ranch.

"Thank you, Dave. I just didn't want to be alone," Bettina said. Some of the lightness had returned to her voice and he guessed she was about over the initial shock of Nathan King's death.

"Obliged for the company," he replied.

They continued on through the warm windy

night, letting the bay pick its own pace, an easy walk that increased in speed only when it came in sight of the ranch. The gelding was tired and hungry and wanted only to reach the corral where feed and rest awaited.

Dave swung the horse toward the house as they entered the yard. Drawing to a halt at the porch, he slid from the saddle skirt, took the rifle from the woman, and reached up to help her down. At that moment the sound of hoof-beats on the road reached them. Immediately Dave pulled Bettina off the bay and pushed her toward the door.

"Inside. Close the door and bar it," he ordered in quick, crisp words as he handed the weapon back to her.

"You think it's those Regulators? The trouble's all over. The army—"

"Could be a bunch that haven't got the word yet. Or it might be some outlaws," Gunnison said, and hunched low, hurried across the yard to the end of the corral from where he would have a clear view of the road.

19

It was Jubal Phillips.

Dave, standing in the deep shadows along the corral, lowered the rifle he had taken from his saddle and held level at the approaching rider. He had been on the verge of triggering a shot when Phillips' slouched shape became more distinct in the pale light.

"Jubal," he called, stepping out into view. "Was about to shoot you."

"Was aiming to sing out," the old cowhand replied as he rode up to Dave and halted. "Figured maybe you all was still a mite jumpy, not knowing the war was over. It all right if I turn my horse into the corral? Aim to ask Nathan if I can have my job back."

"Nathan's dead. So's Dutch," Gunnison said flatly.

Jubal came slowly off his saddle. "Aw, hell," he said in a gusty sort of voice. "Was it them damned Regulators?"

"Far as we know. Found them strung up in that grove of trees near town. Had tags hanging from their boots saying they were rustlers."

"Would've been that Regulator bunch, all right. Outlaws wouldn't've hung no signs from them," Jubal said as they moved toward the corral gate. Dave's bay was there now, having wandered over of his own will, and stood waiting to have his gear removed. "Is Nathan's missus taking it all right?"

"She's the strongest woman I've ever seen—and she'll be glad you're back," Gunnison said, taking care of his horse. "And so am I. Maybe this so-called war's over, but I still expect trouble."

"Bound to last a while longer. Word that the army's moved in ain't got around yet," Jubal said as he turned his horse into the corral. "Big reason I come back. Figured I owed it to Nathan and his missus to let them know how things are stacking up. We best—"

"Wait until we get into the house. Bettina ought to hear it, too."

Jubal said no more and, closing the corral gate, followed Dave across the hardpack to the house.

Bettina heard them coming and was waiting at the door. When she saw Phillips, tears flooded into her eyes. "He's dead, Jubal," she said, choking back her sobs. "They've killed him."

The old cowhand took her into his arms and patted her gently on the shoulder. "I'm sure mighty sorry, I sure am. He was a fine man. Maybe if I hadn't got so het up and rode off like I did, it wouldn't have happened."

Bettina drew back, brushed at her eyes with a corner of the apron she was wearing. "No, it wouldn't have made any difference. They were out to get even with him. Don't blame yourself. It was bound to happen, I guess."

"Yeh, maybe so. It's sure happened to a lot of other folks around here, but you just don't think it'll happen to you or somebody real close."

Bettina turned away, motioning toward the table. "The coffee's hot. If you'll sit down, I'll pour you both a cup. I've had all I can stand."

Dave and Jubal settled themselves in chairs. The older man cocked his head and looked shyly at the woman.

"It all right with you if I take back my old job again? Dave's said it's fine with him."

"It's fine with me."

"We can use all the help we can get," Dave said. "Need to keep an eye on the herd—they raided it, killed off a half-dozen head—and now that Nathan and Dutch are out of it, they'll likely take it in mind to move in and try to burn the place down. . . . What was it you had to tell Nathan?"

"That all hell's busted loose around here now. A fellow that was hanging around the old T-A Ranch, where them Regulators've holed up making out like he was one of them, rode into town a while back. Told the sheriff that a regular army of them Regulators was planning to raid Buffalo, claiming it weren't nothing but a nest of rustlers, and anyone there that didn't side with the Major and them was against the cattlemen."

"Heard in town that the army had finally stepped in," Dave said.

"Yeh, the colonel got the word from the higher-ups that he was waiting for, and headed out to meet the Regulators before they could reach town. Meantime, the whole place was up in arms. The sheriff weren't too sure about the army, so he made up an army of his own. Called for volunteers to stop the Major and his bunch. Got them, too: cowhands, store clerks, homesteaders—anybody that could shoot a gun."

"They know they were going up against a bunch of gunmen?"

"Reckon they did, and they took off armed to the teeth. The merchants there opened up and let anybody that didn't own a gun help themselves to whatever they figured they needed in shooting irons and cartridges. . . . If you was in town, didn't you hear all about it?"

"We were looking for Nathan and Dutch and in a big hurry. Lockhart, the storekeeper, did tell us the army had stepped in, but we didn't learn much more than that."

"Well, I expect it's all over now—at least the army's stopped the Major and his crowd. But there's still a bunch of them running loose stealing and burning—outlaws mostly, I expect—and it's all being blamed on them Regulators. Now, I sure ain't got no use for them, but they're getting credit for a lot of devilment they didn't do."

"All adds up to the same terrible thing," Bettina said. "One bunch of murderers is just as bad as another."

Jubal nodded. "Yes'm, and while the sheriff and the army's all tied up fighting the Major's outfit, things'll be all the easier for the outlaws. It'll be like shooting fish in a barrel for them the next couple of days."

"Not going to make it that easy for them around here," Dave said. "Aim to be waiting for them. We've moved the herd close—into that little hidden hollow east of here—so's it won't be hard to keep any eye on the cattle. About all that's left to be done is fort up." He paused, pointed to the extra guns and ammunition Nathan King had laid out on the table by the window. "We can shoot it out with them for about as long as they want."

"What about fire?" Jubal asked.

"Only thing we can do about that is keep them away from the house."

"That won't be hard," Bettina said. "There are windows on all four sides."

"Four sides—but only three of us," Dave commented, "but I reckon we can manage. One thing, we best clear things away from the windows so we can get to them easy. But first off I think we ought to bury Nathan and Dutch. Might not get another chance for a while. That all right with you, Bettina?"

"Yes, of course, but hadn't you better get a little rest?"

"Be time for that later, once we're all set. You got some place special where you'd like Nathan put?"

"There's a place out behind the barn," the woman replied. "Jubal knows where it is. There are some other graves there. . . . Do you have to do it now?"

"I figure it ought to be done before daylight, before we might be getting some company. You want us to call you when we've finished?"

"No need," Bettina said, her voice low and filled with sadness. "I was with him earlier and said all the things that were in my heart."

Dave, with Jubal at his heels, turned and hurried out into the crisp, early morning. Crossing to the barn, they entered, finished closing Nathan King's coffin, and then carried it and Dutch Hollander's to the small plot of ground marked by a circle of whitewashed stones, a short distance west of the barn and other structures.

Obtaining spades from the toolshed, they fell to digging the graves in the moist, soft ground, and within an hour or so had the trenches, not as deep as they might have been, ready for the coffins. As they lowered Nathan King into one, movement off to the side caught Dave's eye. Instantly his hand went to the six-gun on his hip and then slowly fell away.

Bettina had changed her mind. She stood a dozen paces away, a slight, lonely shape in the fading moon and star light, looking on. Dave studied her for a time and then, when she gave no indication of coming nearer, he picked up the spade he was using and with Jubal began to fill in the grave. When that was finished, they accorded Dutch Hollander the same treatment.

"I'll rig up markers tomorrow, if I get a chance," Dave said as they turned to go.

Bettina had come about also and was moving slowly toward the house. It was just first light and the heavens to the east were beginning to brighten. Abruptly she halted, turned to them. "I want to thank you, both of you," she said. "Nathan would have appreciated all—"

She broke off as the pounding of running horses coming in from the east reached them.

Dave reacted instantly. Tossing the spade aside, he seized Bettina by the hand and began to run for the rear entrance of the house. Nearby, Jubal broke into a run also, and in a small tight group they raced across the yard.

When they reached the door, Dave, heaving for breath as were the others, yanked it open and pushed Bettina inside the house. The hammer of horses' hooves on the hardpack was in their ears as he hurried Jubal through the doorway also. Following quickly, he slammed the thick panel shut, drew his gun, and wheeling to the window, faced the yard.

Newt Thomas made his way through the congestion of Buffalo residents filling the street and mounted the steps to the landing of Lockhart's General Store. The town was in an uproar, alive with rumors as to how the confrontation between the sheriff-led town posse, the army, and the Major's Regulators had gone.

It wasn't his fight, Newt assured himself; he was there to track down and arrest the outlaw, name still unknown, who had participated in a bank robbery in Cheyenne—one that had failed insofar as any large amount of cash was concerned. Apprehending the outlaw and taking him back to Cheyenne was a must that grew in importance with each passing day to the young deputy, for it meant the realization of his hopes, his ambition: the sheriff's star.

Lockhart, the storekeeper, came forward as Newt entered, rubbing his hands together and a frown on his face. "If you're looking for free ammunition, Deputy, I—"

"I'm looking for information," Thomas cut in coolly. "I'm not part of the posse. . . . That man and woman who were just in here, mind telling me who they are?"

A look of relief crossed the merchant's face. "Oh, I see. Well, that was Nathan King's wife. She was here looking for him."

"The man—who was he?"

"Name's Dave Gunnison. One of King's hired hands."

Thomas stirred in disappointment. Gunnison fit the description of the bank robber almost exactly, yet if he worked for somebody named King, and had for some time, then he couldn't be the missing outlaw.

"He been with these Kings long?"

Lockhart shrugged, drew a pipe from his apron pocket, and began to fill it from a paper sack of tobacco. The shouting in the street seemed to have grown louder and the dust swirling above the crowd all but obscured the lamps.

"Ain't sure," the storekeeper said hesitantly. "I ain't never seen him before, sure of that."

The lawman's hopes lifted. This Dave Gunnison could be his man, after all—but there was no real assurance of it. The fact that he was not a long-time employee of the King's could mean nothing; as someone had mentioned, the country was overrun with strangers.

"Obliged to you," Newt said, his voice heavy as he turned for the door.

"You're obliged, I'm sure," Lockhart replied. "Maybe if you'd tell me what you're wanting, I could be of help. Can tell you Mrs. King was mighty upset about her husband. Seems he was missing."

"My business has nothing to do with that," Thomas said, and stepped out onto the landing. As the door closed behind him, he caught sight of Deputy Cullen hurrying toward him, a fold of paper in his hand.

"Thomas," the lawman called, waving the bit of paper—a letter, Newt saw—over his head as he reached the landing. "I reckon this here's that message from Cheyenne you've been looking for."

Thomas hurried to the edge of the platform, took the envelope from the deputy, and ripping it open, tipped the sheet it contained to the light from one of the lanterns hanging from posts at the edge of the landing.

A glow of satisfaction filled him, brought a half-smile to his lips. The message was from Sheriff Dawson. The name of the man he was tracking was Dave Gunnison. Someone had recognized him. He wouldn't have the five hundred dollars on him, however; one of the clerks had confessed he had pocketed the pack of currency and blamed its loss on the outlaws. But bring in Gunnison anyway. He was guilty of attempted bank robbery, and in Wyoming that was a serious crime.

"Good news?" Cullen asked when Thomas stepped down and joined him in the dust of the street.

"Sure is," Newt answered. Sangaree Dawson could start unpinning his star and getting ready to move out of the sheriff's office.

"How do I get out to Nathan King's place?" he asked.

He'd take a ride out there, come morning, and take Gunnison in charge.

20

There were eight of them. In the half-light Dave could see they were all hard-looking, roughly dressed, heavily armed, bearded men. They could be Regulators or they could be outlaws; it didn't matter—both had the same purpose in mind.

A thickset man on a black horse in the center of the party pushed his hat to the back of his head as they all gathered at the edge of the hardpack.

"Ain't nobody here but that corn-shucker's wife—and where he is now, he sure ain't going to be no problem."

Dave heard Bettina's sharp intake of breath. He swore silently. These were the men who had lynched Nathan and Dutch, had come now to ransack and then burn down the rancher's house.

"You sure she's alone?" one of the men asked.

"Reckon I am. We strung up one of the hired hands and the other'n quit. This'll be a easy one."

"Them murdering damn hellions," Jubal muttered, picking up one of the rifles. "I'll fix him so's—"

164

Dave waved the older man back. "Not yet."

"Beaver, you and Amos go inside and drag the woman out here," the heavyset man said.

"Been told she's quite a looker. Young, too," one of the men dismounting commented.

"Can see about that later—after we've gone through the house. From the looks of the place, it ought to be pretty rich pickings. Get a move on."

"Sure enough, Morg."

His .45 in hand, Dave reached for the door latch. Pausing, he glanced over a shoulder at Jubal and Bettina. The woman had a rifle in her hands and was holding it in a familiar, confident way. She was no stranger to the weapon, that was certain. Jubal, too, had his rifle ready.

"Don't shoot unless they force us to," Gunnison said quietly. "They think Bettina's alone. Maybe I can bluff them into riding on. I'm afraid if we just open up on them, it'll only bring more of their bunch. . . . Best you blow out that lamp, Jubal."

Phillips turned to the table, cupped a hand around the top of the glass chimney, and extinguished the small flame with a gusty blast of breath.

In the semidarkness Dave opened the door and stepped out onto the porch. Jubal and Bettina were close on his heels. He would have preferred the woman had stayed inside, but there was determination in the set of her chin, and he knew it would be useless to argue with her even if he had the time.

The two men assigned to enter the house and bring out Bettina were moving away from their horses. They pulled to a startled halt as Dave, flanked by Bettina and Jubal, suddenly confronted them.

"Back off," Dave barked sharply.

One of the pair slowly raised his arms. The other half-turned to Morg as if wanting to know what the outlaw leader wanted him to do.

"Get back on your horses and ride out," Dave continued, his voice taut and barely controlled. "I know you're the bunch that murdered this lady's husband, Nathan King, and his friend. Either of you—or any of the rest of your bunch—makes a wrong move and you're both dead."

Morg, his whisker-covered features indefinite under the shadow of his hat, glanced about as if assessing his strength and possibilities. After a bit he nodded.

"All right, you all are holding the guns. Amos, you and Beaver come on back."

The two men on foot wheeled slowly and began to retrace their steps. Reaching their horses, they swung aboard and took up the lines.

"And don't try coming again," Jubal Phillips warned, " 'cause we'll be all cocked and primed for you."

Morg laughed and glanced about at his men. Over in the chicken yard a rooster crowed lustily, and several of the hogs were squealing as they awaited their feeding.

"Oh, we'll be back, old man," the outlaw said. "Fact is, we ain't even leaving!"

"Look out," Dave yelled as the riders abruptly went for their guns.

He fired from the hip, at the same moment backing toward the doorway of the house. Bettina was to his left, Jubal to his right. Both triggered their weapons at the same moment.

In the unexpected burst of smoke and gunfire two of the outlaws sagged in their saddles and fell to the ground.

"Inside!" Dave shouted, emptying his pistol at Morg and the other outlaws, surprised by the unexpected opposition and milling about in confusion. Backing toward the door with Jubal and Bettina behind him, he jerked the rifle from the woman's hands and began to fire it at the outlaws, now beginning to make use of their weapons. A man near Morg yelled in pain and, clinging to his saddle horn as one of Dave's bullets drove into him, spurred away.

At once Morg and the remaining outlaws, trailed by the mounts of the dead riders, wheeled about and rushed back across the yard in the direction of the barn. Dave continued to lever the rifle he held until it was empty, but the men were bent low and moving fast and erratically. In only moments they reached the structure and were behind it.

"I reckon we showed them," Jubal crowed as he shut the door behind Dave. "You reckon they've had enough?"

Gunnison dropped the crossbar into its brackets, securing the thick panel, and stepped hurriedly to the window in the back wall.

"Doubt it," he said, peering out into the slowly brightening yard. It was still minutes until sunrise, but first light was bringing definition to the shadows. "Expect they'll try us again."

"And I reckon they won't make a mistake and

try coming at us head-on. This time they'll prob'ly rush us from all sides."

"About what they'll do, but they can see this house is like a fort. No bullet's going to get through these walls."

Jubal moved up close to Dave and looked over his shoulder. "Any sign of them?"

Dave shook his head. "They're back there behind the barn figuring what to do," he said, reloading his pistol. "Let's see that all these guns are loaded." He glanced to the side at Bettina. She had not waited for him to make the suggestion but was already replacing the spent cartridges in her rifle. She looked up, saw his eyes on her.

"Maybe it would be a good idea if I took up a stand at the window in the east wall," she said. "They could circle around—or maybe try to start a fire on what they could figure is our blind side."

"Good idea, all right," Dave said, and as the woman moved off into the hallway for the opposite end of the house, he motioned to Jubal. "Keep an eye out from this window."

"Where'll you be?" the older man said.

"Aim to be moving back and forth between the other two sides. That way we'll have the place covered. Got a hunch they'll be trying fire next to get us out of here."

Jubal nodded his agreement and stepped up close to the window. Silhouetted against the small glass pane, his hawklike features appeared sharp, almost graven.

Pivoting away, Gunnison crossed to the hall and entered the room on the south side of the structure. A chair was underneath the window blocking his access, and kicking it aside, he drew back the curtains Bettina had no doubt made, and looked out. The ground nearby was weedy and a corner created by the extension of the adjoining room was filled with dead clumps of sage and other dry brush blown in by the wind.

An immediate worry stirred Dave. If any of the outlaws got to that side of the house they could easily start a fire. Coming about, he crossed to the north side of the building and entered a room there—a sort of storage area, he saw. Pushing his way to the window and brushing aside a square of canvas that served as a curtain, he put his attention on the outside area. A measure of relief coursed through him. The ground was swept clear by the wind and there was no accumulation of dry brush and litter as was the case to the south.

Dropping back, Dave made his way to where Bettina had taken up a stand. It was the bedroom she and Nathan King had shared—large, comfortable-looking with bed, chairs, carpeted floor, fireplace, and lace-edged curtains on the larger window.

As he entered, the woman was close to the square of glass, her eyes on the flare of yellow and salmon light of sunrise. She looked around as he stepped up beside her.

"Nathan liked to watch the sun come up," she said. There were tears in her eyes as she spoke, and Dave realized he had intruded upon her in a very private moment of memory.

"He said once that people who never take time

to see the sun rise are missing the miracle of watching a new day being born."

Dave nodded solemnly. "He said it right. Was a time when I never paid no mind to such things. Then a few years back, when I was holed up in a cave in Mexico and never saw the sun come up or go down for more'n a week, I realized what I was missing. Like a lot of things we sort of take for granted—you don't come to understand how important they are until you've lost them.... Expect I'd better get back to the other windows."

Dave moved off, going first to the glassed opening on the north side of the house, and then to the one on the south. He remained there for a time, although there was no sign of activity on the part of the raiders. Then an hour or so later, with the sun now up and shining brightly, he rejoined Jubal Phillips.

"Anything stirring?"

Phillips shook his head. "Seen a couple of them ride off, sort of circling like. Expect they was having a look at the other sides of the house. Probably seen you and Nathan's missus standing guard and figured they'd best forget trying to get in that way. I've got a hunch they're waiting for somebody."

"Could be. It'll take a small army to break into this house."

"I'm still worrying about fire," Jubal said. "If they come at us from all sides with torches, I ain't so sure we—"

"We'll stop them," Dave said flatly. "We've got the protection—these walls are a good four inches thick—and they'll be out in the open where we can cut them down easy."

"Yeh, reckon so," Jubal said, laying his rifle on the table and leaning against the wall. "Wonder how the war's going?"

"War? Oh, you mean the showdown between the homesteaders and the Regulators."

"Yeh. Sheriff was aiming to lead his bunch out to the T-A Ranch yesterday at sunup and have it out with the Major and them Regulators. I expect all hell's already busted loose."

Dave stared moodily out into the yard, deserted except for the bodies of the two dead outlaws. Over to the side a solitary crow perched on a fence post, eyed Bettina's chickens busily scratching about in the dirt, while inside the shed the cow was bawling impatiently.

"You're probably right, Jubal," he said after a time. "They're waiting for help—and there're plenty of their kind running around loose on the range—with the sheriff all tied up like he's been. Reckon there's nothing we can do but wait. Be sure you got plenty of shells handy."

Jubal nodded as Dave moved off. Again he visited the windows on the north and south sides of the house and once more returned to where Bettina was standing watch. She greeted him silently, her soft, lovely features emotionless as her eyes asked the question that occupied her mind.

"Nothing doing yet," he said. "Jubal figures they're waiting for help. I agree. Once they think they're strong enough, they'll probably rush us."

Bettina's face clouded. "Do you think we can hold them off?"

Dave made no reply for a long breath and then

nodded. The truth was not necessary at that moment; later it would be.

"Think so. We've got plenty of ammunition—and the walls of this house will stop their bullets."

But there would be nothing they could do if the raiders set fire to the barn and other buildings, Dave knew as he returned to the south window. And they'd be lucky if they could stop a dozen or so riders charging the house with burning torches; one was bound to get through.

Time dragged by. Bettina left her post to make fresh coffee and lay out some light bread and sliced beef in the event anyone got hungry. That done, she returned to her post. Near noon Dave, still at the south window, began to wonder if the outlaws had given up and ridden on. And then Jubal's shout put an end to that hope.

"Here they come! Ten, maybe twelve of them—and some of them are carrying torches!"

21

Pivoting, Dave hurried across the room, entered the hallway, and rejoined Jubal. Gunshots were filling the air, and the dull *thunk* of bullets smashing into the wall of the house was like raindrops on a roof. Bits of glass showered Phillips as the window shattered, causing him to pull back, cursing.

Dave, laying down a rapid fire with his rifle through the now open window, turned to Bettina, who had come up quickly from her post.

"Keep back," he shouted as she moved toward the door.

She shook her head and, removing the drop bar, opened the door slightly. "I can—"

"No—best you take the south side," he shouted. "Lot of brush there."

Bettina wheeled at once and hurried off. Dave, reloading, opened the door further. Jubal was still at the window firing steadily at the riders shipping back and forth across the yard as they poured a continual stream of bullets at the house. Three of them had torches in their hands, but

Jubal's rifle was forcing them to keep their distance.

Keeping low, Dave darted through the doorway out onto the porch and in behind the heavy wash bench Nathan King had built for use of the hired help. The smell of burned gunpowder mixed with dry odor of dust filled the air. And beyond the milling raiders, smoke and flames had begun to bulge from the barn. The realization that the outlaws had set fire to that structure sent a fresh wave of anger and helplessness through Dave.

But there was little he could do about that now. Crouched behind the wash bench and further protected by the waist-high wall of timber that formed the walls of the porch, he continued to shoot at the weaving riders almost obscured now by smoke and dust. He could hear the hogs squealing in their pen and the cow's complaints had become louder. The horses, too, unless they broke out of the corral, would soon be trapped by the rapidly spreading fire.

Reloading the rifle from the handful of cartridges he'd stuffed into a pocket, Dave levered the weapon and drew a bead on one of the riders holding a torch. None of the three had been able to get close enough to the house as yet to make use of the fire they carried, but in the deepening haze that now filled the yard their chances would improve.

Holding tight on the outlaw, Dave squeezed off a shot; yells went up as the man went out of his saddle and hit the ground. The raiders hadn't seen Dave slip out onto the porch and the bullet coming from that quarter was unexpected. Three riders came about at once and, circling slightly to the north, spurred for the rear of the house.

Calmly jacking a fresh cartridge into the weapon's chamber, Gunnison drove a bullet into the rider in the center of the trio, quickly levered the gun again, and knocked a second man from his saddle. The third member instantly veered off, leaving his two companions sprawled on the hardpack with the three already there.

The remaining raiders began now to concentrate on the porch. Bullets thudded into the thick wood and clipped the edges of the wash bench, sending sprays of sharp splinter over Dave. Pinned down by the murderous fire, he could only stay low and, unable to return their shots, wait for the shooting to slacken.

Jubal Phillips was still at the kitchen window. The blast of his rifle was a steady, measured sound—sixteen evenly spaced shots, and then a pause as he picked up another weapon lying on the table nearby, or a longer delay while he reloaded, and then the resumption of shooting. The old cowhand, seemingly fearing most the two remaining outlaws who were endeavoring to move in with flaming torches, was directing his shots at them, forcing both to keep their distance.

But for how long he and Jubal could hold off the raiders Dave could only guess. They had a fairly good supply of ammunition; however, forced to throw up a veritable wall of bullets to keep the outlaws at bay, that supply would soon be exhausted.

The firing at the porch and wash bench slackened. Dave, raising his head cautiously, peered over the wall at the raiders. Two more of their number were lying in the dust, downed during the exchange. The advantage of being shielded by Nathan King's thick timber walls was proving far superior to numbers, that was certain.

The barn was burning furiously. Smoke laced with crackling flames was billowing up into the sky. The horses had managed to break out of the corral and were somewhere in the fields below the house. The cowshed was now a small square of fire, the animal herself apparently having succumbed to smoke and heat. No sounds were coming from the chickens and hogs; doubtless they, too, were dead.

Dave turned, hearing the scrape of boots and the closing of a door behind him. Jubal Phillips, hunched low, moved in beside him.

"Can't see enough from inside—the dang smoke and dust being so thick," he said, crouching close to the wash bench. "Here's some more shells," he added, laying an almost full box on the floor between them.

"That all we've got left?" Dave asked.

The older man nodded. "All there is, 'cepting shells for the handguns. Another box of them there on the table."

Jubal began to open up again on the raiders, and Dave, an arm's length or so to the old cowhand's left, resumed shooting. The outlaws had pulled off to the north of the hardpack in deference to the heat the burning barn was throwing off. They seemed content to bide their time, confident the moment would come when they could safely approach the house.

"Expect I'd better see if Bettina's all right," Dave said. "Things have quieted down for a bit."

"I reckon I can hold them if they start up again," Jubal said, feeding cartridges into the magazine of his rifle. "You go right ahead."

"Be back in a minute," Dave said, and on hands and knees crawled back to the door and slipped inside.

Bettina had forsaken the window in the south wall, was standing at the one in the kitchen staring out at the destruction in the yard. Her features were set and there was an angry glint in her eyes. She whirled about as Gunnison entered.

"Those murderers—those killers," she said in a low, hating voice. "I—"

Dave seized her hand and pulled her away from the glassless opening. "Can get hit standing there," he said. "I want you back in one of the rooms where a bullet can't reach you."

Bettina pulled free of his grasp and shook her head. "It's my house—my home. I'm going to help fight for it. Although," she hesitated, looked out again into the hazy yard, "there's not much left to fight for. The barn, the livestock, they're all gone."

"Still got this house," Dave said, glancing toward the doorway as renewed shooting on the part of the outlaws broke out. "Got the herd, too."

"As far as we know we have," Bettina said in a lifeless voice.

The tempo of shooting was rising steadily. Evidently the outlaws had decided to make a move.

"Got to get back to Jubal," Dave said hurriedly, picking up a box of pistol cartridges. "Keep down if you're going to stay in here."

Dropping to his hands and knees again, Dave made his way through the doorway to the wash bench. Jubal, now at the opposite end of the heavily built wooden affair, glanced at him.

"Mighty glad you're back. That bunch is fixing to do something."

"We'll be ready," Dave said, laying the box of cartridges on the floor close by.

"Nathan's missus all right?"

"Was standing at the kitchen window looking out. Made her get back and told her to stay down."

Jubal wagged his head. Sweat glistened on his cheeks and there were powder streaks on his forehead. "Sure is a real shame, all this happening to her. Lost Nathan, now she's losing her ranch."

Jubal was firing as he spoke, uttering the words in between each report of the rifle. Dave began to lay his shots at the outlaws, now widely separated as they crisscrossed the yard in the smoky haze. The barn was now little more than charred remains, as were the other buildings. There was no signs of life insofar as any of the livestock were concerned—even the two dogs that hung around the place lay dead near what had been the corral. Only the cattle had escaped the raiders—and that was only a hope. They, too, could be gone, driven off to be sold to some rancher.

Abruptly the raiders bunched and began to rush the house. Dave, now crowded tight against the front wall of the porch, well protected by the thick timbers, began to trigger his rifle, taking care and picking his targets. The first rider he leveled at threw up his arms and toppled from his horse; the second clutched at his side and cut away. The remaining outlaws didn't slow but came on.

Bullets were again hammering the wall of the porch and the house and smashing the shards of glass remaining in the broken window. Another raider tumbled from his saddle, and one more.

hand clamped to a shoulder, spurred away. The yard had become a shifting wall of thick dust and smoke through which the outlaws and their horses were becoming less visible.

"Hey," Jubal yelled suddenly, springing to his feet. "One of them with a torch has skunt by! Got to stop him before he gets to that brush on the south side."

"Jubal—get down!" Dave yelled in alarm, and triggered his rifle fast in an effort to give the old cowhand a covering fire.

Phillips, weapon blazing, charged on heedlessly, heading straight for the outlaw with the torch. Dave saw the man suddenly wilt in his saddle. The torch fell from his hand and he began to sway drunkenly. Jubal's voice reached Dave through the crackling of gunshots.

"I got him! I got the son of—"

In the next moment Phillips seemed to stumble. The rifle fell from his grasp as he fought to maintain his footing. And then he pitched forward and went full-length on the ground.

Abruptly the door to the house was flung open. Bettina, firing her rifle as fast as she could work the lever, rushed to crouch beside Dave. Her face was drawn and pale, but a fire blazed in her eyes.

"You—you murderers!" she screamed as she poured lead at the raiders.

Her sudden appearance, the deadly fire from both her and Dave coming from behind the invulnerable bulwark of the porch wall and wash bench, and the failure to set the house ablaze appeared to discourage the raiders. Gathering in the far corner of the yard, they held a brief discussion and then, ignoring their dead, wheeled away and were lost to sight beyond the smoldering ruins of the barn.

Dave, Bettina kneeling beside him, watched them go, and when he judged there was no more danger from them he got to his feet.

"Got to see about Jubal. Best you stay put and watch."

Bettina nodded and Dave hurried over to where Phillips lay face down in the dust. He knew before he turned the old cowhand over that the man was dead. Three blood-soaked places on his body marked the location of as many bullet wounds, but he nevertheless walked over to the older man hoping to find a sign of life. It was of no use. The raiders, doing their utmost to cover the outlaw endeavoring to reach the dry weeds at the south end of the house with his torch, had cut Jubal down.

Grim, Dave looked back at Bettina, who was watching him from the safety of the porch, and shook his head. Jubal was number three that the Regulators and the outlaws had killed. But they had paid a hell of a price, he thought, shifting his eyes to the hardpack and the bodies of the dead raiders scattered about. They'd never again—

"Dave!"

Gunnison twisted about to face Bettina. In that same moment he heard the sound of approaching horses. Cursing, he sprinted for the porch. The outlaws were returning.

22

"Back inside the house," Dave snapped urgently, dropping to a crouch behind the bench. "If they start—"

"I'm staying right here," Bettina declared flatly. "Have we got any more cartridges?"

Dave glanced at the box on the floor. It was empty. Shaking his head, he passed the rifle to the woman. "Magazine's near full," he said. "I'll use my six-gun."

Bettina looked out into the yard and the bodies strewn about. "Maybe we can find some shells out there."

"All seemed to be using six-guns. Don't recollect seeing a rifle in the bunch. Too late to look anyway—here they come."

Abruptly a dozen riders broke out into view at the end of the yard—all blue-clad cavalrymen led by a silver bar lieutenant.

"Soldiers," Bettina cried, relief filling her voice. "Late—but welcome."

Dave, a hard smile cracking his mouth, got to his feet and, moving to the opening at the end of the porch, stepped out into the yard. Immediately the officer and his men swung toward him, guiding their horses carefully so as not to trample any of the dead outlaws.

"I'm Lieutenant Wilger," the officer said, pulling to a halt in front of Dave and Bettina. "From Fort McKinney. Storekeeper in town said he thought you might be having some trouble out here so the colonel sent me and some troopers out to have a look. Appears you've got the situation well in hand yourselves."

"Could have used you and your men ten minutes ago," Dave said. "What was left of the outlaw bunch that hit us have gone."

"Which way?" Wilger asked.

"West, I think—leastwise they headed out in that direction."

Wilger raised himself on his saddle and half-turned to face a slim, gray-haired, bristly mustached man. "Sergeant Akins, pick three men, load these bodies on their horses, and take them to town."

"Yes, sir, and what will the lieutenant be doing?"

"I'll take the rest of the men and go after the outlaws. Report that to the colonel when you get back."

"Yes, sir," Akins said, saluted, and barked the names of three troopers. As they rode toward the noncom, Wilger, nodding to Bettina and touching the brim of his campaign hat with a forefinger, shouted a command and led the remainder of the troopers out of the yard at a gallop.

Akins, dismounting, gestured impatiently at the men he'd selected. "You heard the lieutenant! Round up them loose horses and hang these stiffs across the saddles. Hop to it!"

The troopers moved off at once to do the noncom's bidding. Akin himself, pulling off his hat, dusted it across a knee and nodded to Bettina and Dave. A fresh cloud stirred up by the departing cavalrymen was drifting across the hardpack and mingling with the thin smoke rising from the blackened ruins of the barn and other buildings.

"We'll take care of the man lying over there," Dave said, pointing at the crumpled figure of Jubal Phillips.

The sergeant nodded. "He the only one you lost?"

"No, the lady's husband, Nathan King, and another fellow that worked here. Found them last night—murdered. Pretty sure this is the bunch that did it."

Akin smoothed his mustache. "Looks like you made them pay a pretty price for what they done."

"Not near enough," Bettina said. "This house is all that's left of the ranch. Is the trouble all over?"

"Yes'm, except for running down a few individual bunches—like this one you had trouble with."

"Then the army's taken over—broken up the gang they called the Regulators?" Dave asked.

"Them, and that army of homesteaders, too. We got there just in time yesterday to keep it from being a massacre. The homesteaders had loaded up a wagon with dynamite and gunpowder and were aiming to set it afire and roll it down into the house where the Regulators had forted up. We were able to stop them. The colonel then grabbed the leaders of both sides and is taking them back to stand trial."

A sob escaped Bettina's throat. "If only the army had taken a hand a day ago," she cried. "Nathan would be alive—and so would Jubal and Dutch."

The sergeant made no comment, simply watched as his men, the outlaws' horses rounded up, began to load the stiffening bodies across their saddles and cinch them down for the ride back to Buffalo.

When they had finished the chore, Akin turned back to Bettina and Dave. "There anything more we can do for you folks? Be glad to take care of your friend there, and then escort you into town if you like. Maybe it's not safe here, and probably it won't be till we get all of the outlaws caught and behind bars."

Dave glanced at Bettina and then back to the cavalryman. "Expect the lady'll want to stay. She feels pretty strong about the place. Besides, she's got a herd of cattle that'll need looking after—if it's still where I left it."

"Yes, I'll stay." Bettina had moved back onto the porch. Her features were quiet, and she had pushed her hair, which had come loose during the fight, to the back of her neck. She was in complete control of herself again after giving way to her moment of bitterness.

"Whatever you want, ma'am," Akin said, and turning to his horse, swung up into the saddle. Raising his hand, he shouted, "Move out," and led the party off the hardpack, past the smoking remains of the corral, and onto the road to town.

Dave watched the soldiers leave and then turned to Bettina. "I'll bring Jubal up here to the porch, then I'll see if I can scare up enough boards to make him a coffin. If I can't, we'll have to wrap him in his blanket and—"

"Jubal deserves better than that," Bettina said. "There's an old wardrobe cabinet in the storage room. We can use it."

Dave nodded and, moving off to where Jubal Phillips lay, bent down, picked up the slight form of the old cowhand, and started back to the house.

Midway he halted. A rider had appeared suddenly at the edge of the hardpack—a man on a buckskin horse and wearing a fringed coat and a hat with a snakeskin band. Sunlight glinted on the star pinned to his shirt.

The world seemed to come to a halt in that moment for Dave Gunnison. Newt Thomas had caught up with him—and at a time when he could do nothing about it.

23

Head down, Dave ignored the lawman and, carrying Jubal Phillips' body, continued onto the porch. He was cornered; there was no possible way he could escape the lawman now.

Reaching the house, Dave laid the old cowhand alongside the wall of the porch. Without looking up, he knew that Thomas had ridden across the yard and, gun out, was now sitting on his horse a stride or so away.

"Stand up," the deputy ordered. "And keep your hands where I can see them."

Dave straightened slowly. He heard the door to the house open and then Bettina's voice reached him through the hush.

"What is it? What's the matter?"

"Lady," the lawman said quietly, "you'll oblige me greatly if you'll step out into the yard where I can see you."

Bettina's features stiffened. "Who are you? What do you want?"

"I'm Deputy Sheriff Newton Thomas from down Cheyenne way. I've chased this outlaw

186

over half of Wyoming—and he's my prisoner,"
the lawman replied, dismounting.

Bettina moved slowly out onto the porch and
then down into the yard, her eyes filled with a
mixture of concern and anger. "Are you certain
he's the right man you're after?"

"I am."

"What did he do?"

"He and three others tried to rob a bank in
Cheyenne," Thomas replied. "Others are all
dead—he's the only one left. What they done was
all for nothing. They didn't get any money."

"Then why do you have to arrest him?"

"He tried to rob a bank, that makes him an
outlaw."

"No, he's not an outlaw—not really," Bettina
declared, her voice strong and insistent. "If he
had been, he wouldn't be here now. He would
have joined up with all those other outlaws who've
been stealing and killing."

"Maybe so, ma'am, but—"

"And he wouldn't have stayed here helping
my husband before he was murdered and then
helping me afterward. No outlaw would do that."

"I sure don't know about that," Thomas said
stubbornly. "All I know is that he broke the law,
and I have orders to take him back to Cheyenne
to stand trial."

"You'll be putting a good man on trial if you
do, one who deserves better. You can ask the
army how he stood by me when we were raided
by outlaws. Lieutenant Wilger—he was just
here—he can tell you. Maybe he was in on the
robbery—"

"Attempted robbery. I just learned that there was no money taken."

"That proves he's no outlaw," Bettina said triumphantly. "Not down deep, anyway. I expect he just got caught up in it with those other three men. Was anybody in the bank killed?"

"No, only one of the outlaws. Two more were killed south of here a ways, and—"

"You'll be making a terrible mistake if you take Dave back and put him in prison," Bettina continued, her words coming out in a rush. "Do you know that he and Jubal Phillips, the man lying there dead, stood off a dozen or more outlaws who were trying to rob and kill us? You can see what they did manage to do—burn down my barn and kill off most of my livestock. If he actually was an outlaw, do you think he would have stayed here risking his life for two people he'd only known a couple of days?"

Dave, silent through it all, felt a surge of pride as he listened to the defense Bettina put up for him. But he doubted it would have much effect on the lawman. Newt Thomas, as his stubborn determination to track him down indicated, was likely not one to back off.

"I'm real sorry, Mrs. King—that's your name, I think—but the law's the law. Maybe Gunnison there is a good man like you claim, but he broke the law—"

"Law—fiddlesticks! Where was the law when all those real outlaws were riding around the country, killing folks, burning down houses and barns, and destroying stock, all the things we've spent years building up? The law should have been out after them, not looking for a man like

Dave, who's done nothing but help. Why, he actually was out doing the law's job."

Thomas frowned, brushed his hat to the back of his head. He seemed uncertain, disturbed by what Bettina King was saying, but no doubt the oath that bound him to his duty was having its strong way with him.

"If you take Dave, you'll leave me with nobody. My husband's dead; the men who worked for us, except for him, are dead, too; and you can see by just looking around what I'm faced with. Is it the reward from capturing him that you're thinking of?"

"Reward? I—"

"I don't have much money in the house, but I can sell some of my cattle—if I still have a herd—or I'm sure the bank will make a loan."

"There's no cash reward for him, lady. It's something else, a different kind of reward, sort of personal one," Thomas said. He was silent for several moments, and then his shoulders stirred and a wry smile twisted his lips. "But I reckon it ain't all that important." The lawman turned to Dave as he slid his gun back into its holster. "I reckon it won't hurt none to let you go, Gunnison, seeing as how nobody at the bank got shot up and there wasn't no money stolen. Can put your hands down."

A smile crossed Bettina's face and her eyes brightened. "If you do, Deputy—I'll be so grateful!"

"Not living up to my oath," the lawman said, "and it's going to cost me plenty. But I expect another chance'll come along to take over Dawson's job."

Dave glanced at Bettina and then back to Thomas. "Meaning what?"

"Nothing concerning you—just that personal reward I mentioned," the lawman said, and turned back to his buckskin. "One thing, if it ever comes up, you don't know me. Understand?"

"Sure do, Deputy. And I'm obliged to you."

Thomas nodded and swung away. "Thank the lady. She made me see that sometimes the law has to bend a little if it's going to be just. So long."

"So long, and good luck," Dave answered, and crossed to where Bettina was standing. There were tears of relief and joy in her eyes.

"Sure owe you plenty, all right," he said, "and I don't know how to thank you. If it hadn't been for you, I'd probably be on my way back to Cheyenne—and the pen—right now."

Bettina shook her head. "I couldn't bear the thought of you leaving me, Dave. You will stay, won't you?"

"Long as you want me to."

"That could be forever—"

He grinned. "Just what I was hoping to hear."

Ray Hogan is an author who has inspired a loyal following over the years since he published his first Western novel *Ex-marshal* in 1956. Hogan was born in Willow Springs, Missouri, where his father was town marshal. At five the Hogan family moved to Albuquerque where Ray Hogan still lives in the foothills of the Sandia and Manzano mountains. His father was on the Albuquerque police force and, in later years, owned the Overland Hotel. It was while listening to his father and other old-timers tell tales from the past that Ray was inspired to recast these tales in fiction. From the beginning he did exhaustive research into the history and the people of the Old West and the walls of his study are lined with various firearms, spurs, pictures, books, and memorabilia, about all of which he can talk in dramatic detail. Among his most popular works are the series of books about Shawn Starbuck, a searcher in a quest for a lost brother, who has a clear sense of right and wrong and who is willing to stand up and be counted when it is a question of fairness or justice. His other major series is about lawman John Rye whose reputation has earned him the sobriquet The Doomsday Marshal. 'I've attempted to capture the courage and bravery of those men and women that lived out West and the dangers and problems they had to overcome,' Hogan once remarked. If his lawmen protagonists seem sometimes larger than life, it is because they are men of integrity, heroes who through grit of character and common sense are able to overcome the obstacles they encounter despite often overwhelming odds. This same grit of character can also be found in Hogan's heroines and, in *The Vengeance of Fortuna West*, Hogan wrote a gripping and totally believable account of a woman who takes up the badge and tracks the men who killed her lawman husband by ambush. No less intriguing in her way is Nellie Dupray, convicted of rustling in *The Glory Trail*. Above all, what is most impressive about Hogan's Western novels is the consistent quality with which each is crafted, the compelling depth of his characters, and his ability to juxtapose the complexities of human conflict into narratives always as intensely interesting as they are emotionally involving. His latest novel is *Soldier in Buckskin*.